MW00961705

AD ASTRA

ADVENTURES OF THE STARSHIP SATORI 1

KEVIN MCLAUGHLIN

ROLE OF THE HERO PUBLISHING

Copyright © 2013, 2017 by Kevin O. McLaughlin

All rights reserved.

No part of this book may be reproduced in any form or by any electronic or mechanical means, including information storage and retrieval systems, without written permission from the author, except for the use of brief quotations in a book review.

This is a work of fiction. Any resemblance to actual persons living or dead, businesses, events, or locales is purely coincidental.

"Ad Astra Per Aspera"
("A rough road leads to the stars", from the Apollo 1 Memorial.)

ONE

D an tapped each dead soldier in the neck in turn, counting his kills for the evening. He came to six. Add in the bottle he was drinking, and he'd be at seven. That was still under budget. He figured this for a twelve-pack night. Not that the drinking had done him much good. It hadn't numbed the pain he felt. Neither the ever-present ache in his spine or the stabbing sense of loss he felt in his heart. Seven clearly hadn't been enough beers. He'd have to do better than that to dull his senses tonight.

He waved to the woman tending the tables, a middle-aged matron whose name he hadn't tried to catch. Why bother? It was just another random stranger in another dirty bar. He'd been in enough of them lately that they all looked the same to Dan. She'd made a few attempts to clear his growing pile of bottles away earlier in the evening, but he'd shooed her off. Dan wanted the physical memory of the drinks sitting right there, like a badge. The woman saw his wave, but didn't bother coming over. She just went to fetch another beer. He kept his eyes off her face. He didn't want to see her disdain, or worse, her pity.

Instead he brought his eyes back to the bar's TV, where the Ares rocket was still sitting on the launch pad. The countdown was frozen at four minutes and fifteen seconds. It hadn't moved for most of an hour now, last minute problems delaying the launch. That wasn't unusual. Even a small problem could cause a disaster with a mission like this one. The delay was drawing out Dan's agony in a way that made the evening even more excruciating than he'd expected it to be.

"Hey Joe, can we switch the channel? Missing the game here," a burly man seated at the bar called out to the bartender.

"Yeah, Joe. This shit is boring," said another heavy-set guy seated next to him.

Both of them were lumberjack big, wearing dirty work clothes. The sort of rough and tumble types who would be unlikely to back down from an argument, and quick to turn one into a fight. None of which bothered Dan even a little. Maybe if he'd been a little less drunk, he would have let them have their way. But perhaps not. Retreat wasn't in his nature, either.

"Don't touch that channel," Dan snarled.

"Or what?" asked the first man. He half rose from his seat as he turned toward Dan.

"Wanna find out?" Dan said, managing to slur his words only a little bit.

"Man, don't mess around. Who wants to see this stupid rocket sitting there, anyway?" the guy replied. "It's not even going anywhere."

"I do," Dan said.

"Larry, you can't pick a fight with a gimp," the guy's buddy whispered to him, loud enough that Dan could hear anyway.

Larry blushed and sat back down, finally noticing Dan's wheelchair and the uniform he wore. "Hey, man, sorry. You can watch what you want."

Dan felt a pang of guilt over the other man's mistake. He saw a soldier in uniform, seated in a wheelchair, and thought he was looking at some veteran wounded in combat. The truth was nowhere near so exciting. He was an Air Force major, all right. For at least the next few days, until the medical discharge was finalized. But he hadn't been hurt by a missile or gun. It hadn't been a training accident or enemy action that did him in. No, it was his own conscience that had stuck him in this chair for the rest of his life.

The bartender glared at Dan for a moment from behind his glasses, wiping furiously at a mug with a dishrag. The guys at the bar must be regulars, Dan figured. He probably knew them both by name, and he was pissed at how Dan had acted. But the TV stayed on the same channel despite what the local crowd wanted, so that was all right. There were plenty of bars. This launch was only going to happen once.

Finally the countdown started up again. Whatever the problem was, they must have solved it. There were four minutes left, and the seconds were ticking away. Unconsciously, Dan activated his motorized chair and moved toward the TV. Three minutes left. God, this sucked. Why was he doing this? It would have hurt less to stay home and pretend the launch wasn't happening. But he couldn't take his eyes from the screen, no matter how much it pained him to watch.

His eyes misted a little as the first plumes of

steam appeared under the titanic rocket. The payload was a crew compartment and landing vehicle – and the first six humans from Earth to ever attempt bridging the vast distance to Mars. They'd be traveling for six months to get there, stay for six months, and then return. It was the adventure of a lifetime. It was supposed to have been the adventure of his lifetime.

He slugged down the last of the beer he was still holding. The bitter flavor matched how he was feeling. The matron plunked his new bottle down where he'd been sitting, and he reached for it without thinking, wincing as his back spasmed in protest. He grimaced. Wheelchairs went in reverse for a reason.

Less than two minutes left until takeoff. He leaned forward, willing himself into the cockpit of that ship with everything he had. He should have been there. Would have been there, if it hadn't been for a random accident. There was something ironic about being taken down by a mini coupe after surviving dozens of missions into space unscathed. He was one of the most experienced space pilots in the world. He'd fought hard to win his berth on that mission.

All gone, now. A driver lost control of his car. A

little kid was crossing the street about six steps ahead of her mom. Dan didn't even think - he just reacted. He rushed out into the crosswalk, body-checking the child clear of danger. She'd been fine. A few bumps and scrapes, but nothing the average six-year-old couldn't recover from. Dan had taken the impact dead on and been hurled twenty feet through the air. He didn't remember much of that, and was grateful for it. The doctors said he'd been lucky to survive at all.

The man who'd smashed into Dan wasn't going to have his license back for a while, but that didn't help heal his badly fractured spine. NASA's policy toward an injury as severe as his had no leeway. As far as they were concerned, he was grounded for good. So he'd taken the early retirement with full benefits and disability that the Air Force had offered. A good deal, but as a consolation prize it sucked. He had some buddies in Panama who told him that income would let him live like a king down there.

If only he could find some reason to live at all.

Fifty seconds left on the countdown. The numbers ticked away on the corner of the TV screen.

With thirty eight seconds left, Dan's phone rang.

The sound startled him, but out of habit he answered it, not taking his eyes off the TV as he did.

"Dan Wynn here."

He watched two more seconds tick away on the countdown before a distorted voice said "Dan! Was hoping to catch you. How're you holding up?"

"Who is this?" Dan asked. He didn't want to talk to anyone.

"It's John," the voice replied, after a short delay.

"John, you have any idea what you're calling in the middle of?"

Another brief delay, and then John said "I'm watching it too, Dan. Why do you think I called you now?" Dan could almost hear his friend's smile over the phone line.

"I think you're interrupting," he said, eyes narrowing. The last thing he needed right now was a pity call. Even from an old friend.

Another pregnant pause. "Dan, I'm calling to offer you a vacation, and maybe a job if you want it. I need people I can trust, and you're top of the list."

"I'm flattered, but–" Dan broke off in mid-sentence as the Ares rocket launched, huge plumes of fire obscuring it from view for a moment before sending it skyward. As it lifted into the sky, all his hopes and wishes vanished with it.

Being a pilot had been his life. Flying things into space had been everything he'd ever dreamed, and more. Now it was gone, all of it. He was a grounded astronaut, lost without anything left in his life that he valued. He couldn't even regret the accident, damn it. Because he'd seen the little girl he saved. She and her parents had visited him while he recovered at the hospital. They'd been crying. The girl gave him a get-well card. And Dan knew that if he had to make the same choice again, he'd do precisely the same thing anyway. Even if saving someone else had cost him everything.

"Dan. DAN." John's voice was still nattering at him on the phone. "Listen to me."

"What?" Dan said. His voice sounded hollow to his ears.

"Vacation, Dan. You need it. And I can use you, if you want to stay on, after."

"I can't," Dan replied. "Still got paperwork to finish my retirement package, and the docs want to see me daily for rehab."

"I've already cleared your paperwork up. Had a general who owed me a favor. And we've got doctors on site who'll continue your rehab. But I need you here, Dan."

The little delays in John's responses finally made their way through Dan's muddled thoughts. A couple of seconds of pause, each time he spoke. It was the same amount of delay. Not a conversational pause, then, but one caused by distance.

"Where are you, John?" he said, curiosity leaking into his voice. He took another sip from his bottle, trying to steady his thoughts.

"I'm on the far side of the moon, Dan. Want to come up for a visit?"

TWO

Dan almost choked on his beer. He'd been expecting...well, something. With John, it was always something. The man was into everything, and had business interests involved across just about every sector of industry Dan could name. But that was one answer he hadn't anticipated. What the hell was John doing on the moon? Dan was so startled that he almost missed the part about John asking him to join him there. In space. He blinked, his mouth suddenly dry. Another sip from his beer solved that and gave him a moment to focus his thoughts again. Was this life's way of giving him a second chance?

"Hell yes, I'll join you," Dan said at last.

Another short pause, then John spoke again.

"Put the drink down and go outside. A car will be waiting for you there. The driver will take you to my launchpad. That is, if you are still interested in going back into space?"

Dan stared a moment at the TV again, where the camera was still following the plume of fire burning its way into the sky. For the first time all day, he could look at the ship without feeling like he was being stabbed through the heart. He still felt a pang watching the ship lift off into the evening sky, but it wasn't accompanied by the same sense of utter hopelessness he'd felt just moments ago.

"I'm on my way," Dan said.

He turned off his phone, slapped enough bills on the table to pay for his beers plus a healthy tip for the scowling waitress, and rolled out toward the door. Halfway there he stopped. He turned the chair around and went back over to the bar, rolling up next to the man he'd yelled at a few minutes before. The big guy looked down at him like he was expecting a second round of snark, but Dan held up both his hands in a peaceful gesture.

"I wanted to say I'm sorry," Dan said. "For being an asshole. It's been a rough few weeks, but that doesn't excuse it."

"No problem, man," the guy - Larry, his name had been - replied. "Keep it real."

Dan nodded to him and turned to leave again. He felt lighter for having made the apology. It wasn't like him to berate someone like that, and it hadn't just been the beer talking, either. He knew John well enough to know that whatever he was calling Dan into space for, it was going to be interesting. He needed to be himself, for this. He needed to find himself again. The apology felt like a good first step.

Dan reached the door and went out into the cool evening air. John was as good as his word. A young driver was already waiting out front, standing outside a large black SUV hybrid with a wheelchair lift built into the side. He expertly hooked Dan's chair up to the device, chatting amiably as he worked.

"The boss was dead on right about you," he said.

"Oh?" Dan replied.

"Yup. Called me, said you'd be out the door within five minutes. Took you three minutes thirty."

"Well. John always did know what buttons to push on people."

"He's good that way. I'm Andy. You're Dan Wynn, the astronaut?"

The simple question rocked Dan. "I suppose...I am. Again."

The driver hooked straps from the vehicle to his chair to hold it in place. A few deft movements, and he was done. Dan was impressed; it usually took the taxi drivers a lot longer to get him situated. This guy knew what he was doing. Dan relaxed some. Cars still made him nervous, especially when he wasn't the one driving them, but he felt like he could trust this driver. Andy tugged the straps a little, checked to make sure they were locked tight, and then slammed the door shut.

Dan caught a glimpse of himself in the rearview mirror and winced. His hair had grown out a lot in the six months since his injury. He hadn't bothered to keep it in a military trim, and now it was a dark, untidy mess. He ran his fingers through it, trying to restore some semblance of order without much success. He sighed and gave up. Short hair was so much easier to manage. Maybe John had a barber out there.

"Boss said to give you these," Andy said as he hopped back into the driver's seat. He passed back a bottle of cold Gatorade and a travel packet of extra-strength Tylenol.

"Thought of everything, didn't the smug..." Dan muttered.

John knew him too well. But he took the drink and the meds. The last thing he needed was to be hung over for a launch. John's little present would help. Dan patted the leg bag hidden in his sweatpants and grimaced. His urine drained there. The docs had said he had enough bladder control to do without one now, and they had been pushing him to ditch the bag for days. But he'd resisted. So much trouble to get into a bathroom, then get up to use it. Too much trouble for someone who'd already given up on living. It was so much easier to just use the bag and Texas catheter. Now he felt embarrassed about the little condom-shaped device and the tube that ran into the hidden bag. He'd been drinking a lot tonight, and his bag was already mostly full.

"Andy, I've got a problem," he said.

"Yeah?"

He winced. This wasn't fun to explain to a stranger. "I need to change out my leg bag. Old one is just about full of processed beer piss. I've got a spare with me, but you got something for the old one?"

Andy passed back a plastic bag. "Cap it, stick it in there and tie it off. Then rest, why don't you? We've got a longish drive ahead."

Dan unhooked the bag and swapped in the new one, capped the old bag, and then placed it into the fresh plastic bag as the driver had suggested. He wasn't sure what to do with the tied-off bag and its contents, so he plopped it onto the floor. It wasn't going to make a mess now, anyway. Dan decided that it was well past time to get over himself and get rid of the leg bag crutch. He popped the Tylenol and leaned back as much as his wheelchair would allow. He gulped down some of the sports drink.

Lulled by the gentle rumble of the vehicle, he fell into the first nightmare free sleep he'd had in weeks.

THREE

John Caraway sat at his desk, looking out over one of the most splendid vistas ever seen by human eyes. The wall screen in front of him wasn't a real window, of course. His office was buried under a thick layer of lunar rock. The entire complex was. Safer that way. The rock served to block both solar radiation and peeping eyes.

But he loved the view, so whenever he wasn't using the screen for something else, he had it set to a live camera on the surface. Right now the sun was dawning over the horizon on the moonscape. It would creep along like that for days, slowly shifting the shadows over the cratered rock. One lunar day/night cycle was about twenty eight Earth days long, so each dawn was something he treasured. Every time he thought he had memorized those patterns, they seemed to surprise him with something new. The two weeks when this part of the moon was turned away from the sun felt interminable, sometimes.

But during the lunar day, he enjoyed sitting there watching the slow creep of light overcome the darkness. He'd hung his wife's picture on the wall to one side of his desk so that they could share the view. He knew Satori would have loved it as much as he did.

An alarm beeped urgently from his console, interrupting his thoughts.

"Majel, display radar to main screen," he said.

"Acknowledged," the computer replied in a woman's voice. John's wall screen changed in an instant to reflect the local radar telemetry. He bounded from his desk for a closer look, skipping over the fiberglass floor in the low gravity. He might be pushing fifty, but on the moon he sometimes felt like a kid thanks to the reduced gravity.

There it was again, the trace of the satellite as its orbit carried it once more toward his base. It would pass almost directly overhead in about ten minutes, according to the display data. He tapped the screen to zoom in on the object.

This was the tenth time in the last three days that particular satellite had zipped by overhead. In fact, the computer analysis of its course showed that it had changed trajectory more than once in order to shift orbits and pass by his base from a different angle. The satellite was ostensibly owned by an Indian mining corporation. John had queried their main office about the device, and been told that it was making survey passes to look for prime sites for launching their own helium-3 operation. Since the first operational fusion reactors had come online a few years ago, mining for helium-3 on Luna had become a high agenda item for a number of nations. It wasn't abundant in the regolith of the moon, but it was impossible to get on Earth in the volumes required to head off the blooming energy crisis. It was probably now the most valuable substance in the solar system. Everyone wanted to stake their own claim in the new 'gold rush'.

Yeah, the satellite could be a survey device. Or that could just be a good cover. John's mining oper-ation was the first one successfully pulling helium-3 from the moon. A lot of folks wcre interested in how he was doing it. Corporate espionage was a real risk, and he had secrets within secrets that he didn't want getting out to the world just yet. If his rivals on Earth had an inkling of the full scope of what he was doing here, there would be a lot more satellites out there.

"Majel, ring General Bennett's office, please? Tell them that satellite is doing another fly-by."

Bennett was his link into the United States military command. His office was the one that had fronted the money for Caraway Industries to start this venture up. John's pitch was a good one: if the Army had first dibs on the helium-3 Caraway pulled out, they'd be set for energy reserves. He made the issue into one of national security – if he didn't get there first, another nation was going to do so. The generals made nice with politicians and got him the money he'd needed that the private sector couldn't afford. Overnight, John had gotten access to every Swiftbow rocket the Air Force could manufacture. At a cost of four billion dollars per launch, the start-up expenses had run into the low twelve digits in launch costs alone.

The energy crisis was bad enough that the generals hadn't blinked.

So in a scant six months, the moon had gone from having no humans on the surface, to his base operational, with a crew of almost a hundred. Already his mining engines were chewing up huge chunks of lunar regolith, grinding it into dust which could be processed into various components. The real gem was the helium-3, of course, but he was hoping to refine plenty of other materials out of the stuff as well. Silicon, aluminum, even titanium could be found in that dust. Some of it he'd use to expand the base, while more valuable bits were dropped back to Earth. One of the first things he'd sent out to the budding base was the biggest digital fabricator he could buy. The thing filled a room here. Even disassembled, it had taken the entire payload of one rocket launch to get it from Earth to the moon.

But that fabricator had been crucial. From the debris left by tunneling out the base, he'd had the machine kick out silicon fiberglass for wall, floor, and ceiling panels. It had manufactured the doors, the furniture, and much more. Digital fabrication had come a long way in recent years – ten years before, hauling all the materials up from Earth would have made a base this big impossible.

Instead, he had the makings of a self-sufficient city on the moon. Solar panels supported their power needs. The mining operation gave them access to minerals which they could then refine into most items through the fabrication machine. The hydroponics level gave them a means to recycle wastes, transform carbon dioxide into breathable oxygen, and fresh vegetables. The only tight spot was water - but the base had been built on top of a cavern filled with water ice. With careful recycling that ice had more than enough to supply their oxygen and water needs for years to come.

Plenty of time to figure out what they were going to do next. This base held secrets which could not remain hidden forever. Sooner or later John knew he would have to reveal what he was developing there to the world at large. He just needed a little more time. Time to show the world what was possible. Time to create a vision that would take humanity into the future.

He watched the satellite cross overhead on his screen and hoped that he would have enough.

FOUR

J ohn's door chimed, bringing his thoughts
back to the here and now. He quickly
checked the hall camera to see who had
arrived and smiled when he recognized her
at once. He'd been expecting this visit.

"Come," he said.

The door split down the middle, each half
sliding into recessed ports on the walls with the
quiet sound of electric motors whirring. He'd built
every door in the base the same. In an emergency,
those would slam shut, keeping atmosphere in
wherever possible for as long as possible. Luna was
a dangerous place, but he'd taken as many precautions as he reasonably could. The base was built to

last, as solid a foundation for his work as engineering could provide.

The woman standing in the doorway paused until the doors had slipped back completely, and then stepped inside his office. The doors slid closed after she'd crossed the threshold. John took one look at her stormy face and tried not to wince. This was not a woman to trifle with on the best of days. Especially so when her temper was up.

"What do you think that satellite is up to now?" she said.

"Hello, Beth. How's the rebuild on our project coming?"

"It's well hidden from that floating spy-cam," she snapped back. "But having satellites zipping by overhead is going to make it very hard for us to do any testing once the construction is complete."

"Nonsense," John said. "We'll make it work. I knew from the start that we were going to attract interest up here. So long as it looks like our work here is all about mining and solar collection, no one's going to suspect anything else is going on. Certainly, no one would guess what we actually have."

Beth frowned. "No, probably not. And the project is buried deep enough that they can't spot it from orbit. But I still worry. Eventually you're going to have to run tests, you know."

"Actually, I plan to do so next week, if you can be ready." He waited calmly for the explosion he knew was coming. Beth didn't disappoint.

"Next week! And when were you planning to tell your lead engineer?" She glared at him, hands on hips.

"I'm doing so now. I said, if you can be ready," John replied. "Can you?"

"Possibly. If we push hard on the final installations and checks. We could maybe manage a week," Beth said. "But that's jumping the schedule up quite a lot. Besides, you still need a pilot, right? Qualified ones aren't exactly easy to come by, not with a dozen governments offering big bucks to them."

"And we need someone we can trust, which makes it even more challenging," John reminded her. "But I've got one."

"Who?" Beth said.

John flashed her a grin. "Guess."

"No. You did not," she said, voice flat and dangerous.

John sighed. This was going to be hard. He wasn't the only one who had a history with the pilot he'd selected. He'd already given up on convincing Beth in the values of this plan. That was why he'd put things in motion before he discussed the matter with her. At the end of the day, John was still the one writing the cheques that kept this place running. It was his base. It was his call.

"I trust him. You even trust him, if you think about it. And Dan's as qualified as you can get. If he hadn't been hit by a car, he'd be on his way to Mars right now," John replied.

"I still think we ought to talk about this more before you–"

"He's on his way here. It's done, Beth. Dan's in."

Her mouth snapped shut in a thin line, her eyes narrowing. John had to struggle to keep from flinching at the flint he saw in her eyes. This whole thing might be a bigger problem than he'd thought. If Beth was this angry, it meant that she still cared. He'd have to watch the situation carefully as it developed, but the die had been cast. He was standing by his decision, damn it.

"Fine. If that's all, then? I have to get back to work if you want me to be ready on your time line," Beth said.

Without waiting for his answer, she turned on her heel and left the office.

John tapped a button on his desk, restoring the view to his camera, and stared out across the moonscape. He was taking a big chance, bringing Dan into the mix, and not just because of Beth's issues. He knew that. But Dan really was one of the best possible solutions to his pilot problem. They'd been friends since college – Dan, a bright youngster with his head in the stars, and he a middle-aged businessman trying to learn about the new frontier, so he could be on the cutting edge when the expected commercial space boom exploded. If there was anyone he could trust to keep a secret, it would be Dan. He needed someone who was very good, and he needed someone he could trust implicitly. Dan filled both needs to a T.

But his friend was damaged goods. John had managed to get a peek at Dan's psych evaluation along with the medical records on his accident. One stroke of bad luck, and Dan had gone from NASA's rising star to being delisted as a pilot and medically discharged from the Air Force.

He clasped his hands behind his back. His friend was hurt more deeply than just the damage to his spine, severe as that was. His pride, his sense of self, his sense of purpose – John knew what it was like to wake up one day without a reason to keep on living. He'd never repay the debt he owed, but maybe he could make a start by giving Dan back that sense of purpose.

A little speck of light flashed by his camera view for a minute; the satellite sliding by the base, taking more pictures to send who-knew-where. So many balls in the air, John thought. And the price for dropping any of them could be catastrophic.

He sat down in his chair again and turned to the picture of his wife, as he often did when he was troubled. Her smile always reminded him why he was here. Satori had wanted to travel into space – to reach out into the beyond as far from the Earth as she possibly could. To her, the vastness of space was not empty, but full of mystery and wonder. But she'd shelved those dreams for a life with him, and then her star had been snuffed out trying to bring their son into the world. He'd thought that her dreams would have died with her.

"But I have carried you into space, my love," he said softly. "And I will make your name remembered, so that no one will ever speak of humanity's journey into the stars without saying it."

FIVE

Dan woke up when the vehicle stopped. He blinked and looked around, feeling more sober after his rest during the ride. He knew this spot well; Andy had driven him to the Florida International Spaceport, the same set of pads from which NASA launched the Mars mission earlier this evening. A Swiftbow IV rocket was already standing in another launch berth a short distance away. It looked ready to go. That had to be his ride. Andy opened the door and reached in to unbuckle him, but he'd already undone the straps.

"Eager to get out there?" Andy said, flashing a knowing grin.

Dan couldn't help but like this man with his easygoing manner and quick smile. He found himself hoping that Andy was more than just ground support for John. Maybe they'd see each other again, out there. Or after he returned. He found himself liking the idea and looking forward to it. That itself felt new to Dan. Looking forward to things was a concept he thought he had given up after the accident.

"Damn right," Dan replied.

"Well, we'll get you loaded right away. You're the only new personnel flying out on this trip. The rest of the payload is supplies for the base," Andy said as he worked the lift to lower Dan's chair back down to the ground.

"Base? How big an operation is John running out there?" Dan asked. And how had he missed hearing about all this? It wasn't like he'd checked out entirely…except he realized that he had. Dan hadn't been keeping up on the news much for the last six months. It hadn't seemed to matter, so he didn't really care.

"You'll see," Andy said.

A man in an orange jumpsuit ran over from the launch pad and moved as if to help with the wheelchair like he was an invalid. Dan cocked an eyebrow at him and engaged the motor, powering past the guy toward his ticket back into space. He might be stuck in a chair, but he could get around on his own just fine. He didn't need someone to push him around. Besides, the motor chair would get him there faster than the guy would push, and he was anxious to be aboard and start this adventure. Half of him felt afraid this was all a dream, and that if he didn't grab the chance fast enough someone was going to come along and tell him that he couldn't go.

"Hey, you'll want this," Andy called to him, holding a tablet in his hand. "Some homework here about John's mining operation. John had me load some books he thought you'd like, too. It's a long flight."

Dan stopped and looked at him intently. With most of the alcohol out of his system, he was better able to take in the man's appearance. Andy was practically made of lean muscle. His blonde hair was slashed short in a cut that wasn't quite military. He wore a white polo shirt and beige slacks, with a casual charcoal blazer to round off the outfit. Andy turned for a moment, and Dan saw the telltale signs of a pistol holstered under his jacket in the small of his back.

"Not going up?" Dan asked.

"Not this time, Mr. Wynn."

"Call me Dan, please. Off to fetch more special projects for John?"

"Something like that," Andy replied noncommittally before heading back to the car and driving off.

An interesting man. Military or a vet, Dan would bet money on that. Probably some sort of combat arms. It was there in the way Andy walked, the careful cadence of step that said he had experience moving with deadly force when he had to. He'd forgotten to ask if Andy would be joining them at Luna or not. Dan hoped he would. He seemed like someone who would be interesting to talk with.

"This way please, sir," the annoying guy in orange said, then started off toward the launch pad. Dan engaged the motor in his wheelchair again and followed, catching back up quickly. They reached the base of the rocket, and the technician inserted a card into a slot, which opened the elevator doors to allow them access. Dan followed him in, and they began gliding their way to the top of the rocket.

He admired the vehicle as they sailed past it toward the capsule. The Swiftbow was a smallish vehicle mostly used to boost commercial satellites into orbit. Light and fast, if a bit bumpy on the takeoff compared to the larger rockets NASA tended to use for astronauts. But today there were four crew on board, including himself. He was last to arrive, so he didn't get a good look at any of them before shifting over to his flight chair.

The same obnoxious tech who'd escorted him in pushed the wheelchair back into the lift before returning to check on him. When he got back he made as if to buckle Dan into the seat, and Dan had to chuckle a little at the look on his face when he saw the straps already expertly done up.

"Kid, I've logged more hours in these rockets than just about anyone else alive," Dan said.

The tech's face lit up with a smile. "I know, sir. Should've known better. I read about what you did."

"Yeah?" Dan said, his expression suddenly guarded. The other man seemed not to notice.

"It was what a hero would do, sir. Glad to see you going back out there." He stepped out of the capsule and closed the hatch.

A hero? Dan had been given that line before. The Air Force had even given him some silly medal or other over the episode. He hadn't felt heroic at the time. He'd just done what needed doing. What he thought anyone would have done if they'd seen a little kid in danger. You help those who can't help themselves. That wasn't heroic. It was just part of being a decent human being.

Wasn't it? Dan worried at the problem for a few minutes, thinking it over without coming to a resolution he was happy with. Then the rumbling of the rocket's engines as they prepared to lift off brought him back to reality. Adrenaline shot through him, same as it always had right before launch. Only this time was even better, more sweet than ever before, because he'd thought that this was lost to him forever.

Ten minutes later, they were off. No delays? Dan was impressed.

Acceleration during liftoff hurt his back, enough pain that it made him bite his lip to keep from swearing.

OK, launch hurt. No shock there. But it was that sort of pulled muscle pain, like when you were trying to work something injured again a little too soon. He had a feeling pulling any serious gees in the future would always at least twinge a little, but he could cope with that. He'd welcome it, if it meant being able to work in space again.

He smiled. He was really doing it. Strapped into the top of this roman candle on steroids, he was going back into space. He'd thought this part of his life was over. Next to that, the pain didn't matter. Neither did not knowing what John was up to – and knowing John, he was up to something...

...and then he was weightless again, and the pain went away. Not just faded, not merely less. Gone. He took a deep breath, exhaled. The pain in his back had been with him ever since the accident. Surgery and rehab afterward hadn't taken it all away, although it had gotten better. Pain medication hadn't taken it all away either. But the weightlessness of space took the pressure off screaming nerves in his damaged spine, and gave blessed relief.

He knew he was grinning like a school kid, but he couldn't help himself. Yeah, John was up to something. And it would be something exciting, something amazing. With John, it always was.

It could even be something worth living for.

SIX

Beth slid down the ladder to the hangar deck, feet dangling free, letting her hands slow her fall in the lunar gravity. She preferred to come down this way from her room on the floor above. Why take an elevator when you can drift down instead? One had to make the most of simple pleasures. Some days being on the moon felt like she was a little kid, sitting in the middle of the best playground ever created. Not that she'd let the people working for her get wind of such ideas. She'd never be able to keep discipline if they knew she had feelings like that.

The huge room was only dimly lit. The work crew was off shift right now. They'd never been able to collect enough techs whom they could trust absolutely to have more than one shift working on the project. This part of the base was deep underground, at the lowest level of the facility. Only a handful of John's staff were permitted access to the area. The retinal scanners in the elevator made sure of that. Secrecy was paramount to the project. If even a rumor of what they were working on got off the base and back to Earth, they'd be sunk.

She really ought to be in bed. They'd all be back at it early in the morning, and there was still much to do if they were going to make John's crazy schedule. But Beth was still fuming inside. Going to bed now would be futile – all she'd be able to think about would be Dan. Coming here. John was good at dropping surprises in her lap, but she resented the hell out of this one. She'd come down here where she would have a little privacy to cool down.

Without thinking about it, she looked down at her left hand, where her ring used to be. When she realized she was looking, she shook her head with a sharp, decisive motion. That was a lifetime ago. She'd treat Dan just as she did everyone else. She hoped he felt the same, and would be able to maintain the same professional detachment she intended to display. If not, that was just too bad. It would be his problem, not hers.

Little pools of illumination from a few emergency lights spilled across the floor in front of her. They partially lit the metal frames around the project – her baby, her night and day obsession for the past few months. She walked a slow circle around the scaffolding, making mental notes about what sort of work had to be prioritized, if she was to have everything ready for next week. The crew was going to hate the rush. But they'd put as much sweat and tears into the work as she had. They'd be willing to put in the hours for a last push. And John was right – time was short. They needed to make this work and get some results worth showing soon. Those satellites floating above them on a daily basis were a clear indication that the world wasn't willing to just leave them alone up on the moon. Others would be coming to set up their own bases. The secret would become more difficult to keep as the weeks wore on.

As she rounded the far end of the scaffolding, she heard a clatter from somewhere behind her in the gloom. The sound of metal clanging against metal echoed hollowly off the stone walls. Beth froze, wary, and then took a few cautious steps toward the sound. This area should be on lockdown during the off shift. No one but she or John should be here.

"Is someone there?" she called, trying for as stern a voice as she could manage.

No response. The darkness in the room seemed to glower at her. She'd never felt nervous in this chamber before, but Beth had the feeling she wasn't alone down there. And she should be.

"Anyone?"

Still nothing. She stopped just outside one of the pools of light. There was plenty of reason for some healthy concern when it came to this job. Every nation on the planet below would be fighting it out for what they had here, if the word got out. That's why John hand-picked every person who was told what was really going on in the depths of his lunar base. Not that the solar power collection and helium-3 mining weren't important – they were. But what he had down here was so much more than that.

"Computer, full illumination," she said in a loud voice. Immediately, lights came on across the ceiling, blanketing the room with bright white light.

The darkness was banished as if it had never been, and polished metal gleamed everywhere in an expansive room, perhaps half the size of a football field and half as tall.

Still, she saw nothing. No movement, no one there at all. She walked through the scaffolding, looking for what might have made the noise, and finally found a small tray of tools scattered on the floor. Someone must have forgotten them, left them out, and they happened to tip over.

"Getting too nervous about this whole thing," she said ruefully. She needed sleep. Between the stress of the schedule and her worries over John's selection as pilot, she was imagining things. A good night of sleep would set her right. Tomorrow they'd begin the final stages of the project.

She collected the tools back into their tray and placed them on top of a large tool bin set around the frame. She'd sort out just where they were supposed to go tomorrow. For now, she needed rest. It was going to be a busy week. But she was excited about what would come after. All of the labor they'd put into this project would finally be realized. Some people down on Earth were going to be very surprised with what they had here, once they were ready for the big reveal. But first they needed to show that it worked, and that meant testing.

A short walk took her back to the ladder, and as she set her hands on the rungs, she said "Computer, lights out." The system obediently bathed the room in shadow again as she began to climb.

SEVEN

The excitement of being back in space had worn a bit thin during the two day journey to the moon, even with the reading material Andy had provided him. The stopover at the International Space Station had been nice, but the trip from there was an uneventful cargo shuttle ride. Dan still couldn't suppress a grin as he wheeled his new chair down the shuttle ramp into the bay. The old motorized beast had been left behind on Earth; too much expense to lift it into space. Instead, as soon as his ride had landed on the moon a nurse had rolled in with a new chair, all plexiglass and aluminum, built on site. Probably built specifically for him. No motor meant he had to wheel it around himself, but the gravity was so light here that it wasn't really a bother. If anything, he had a feeling he'd have to watch out not to push too fast and lose control.

The chair was nice, but his grin was for John, standing there in the hall ahead of him and practically dancing from foot to foot in excitement. He was always like that when he was eager to show off some new toy or pet project. And his enthusiasm was always catching, so Dan found himself feeling that familiar eagerness spread through him as well. Whatever John was involved in up here, it had to be exciting to light that fire behind his friend's eyes.

"Dan, good to see you!" John reached out and pumped Dan's hand.

"You too, John. Thanks for inviting me up. You're right, this was amazing. Just what I needed."

"You don't know the half of it. But I could really use your help, if you're willing," John said.

"I figured you weren't going to the expense of hauling me up here for a joy ride." He'd hoped as much, anyway. Dan could have lived with the trip if it was really just a pity vacation. Being back in space felt that good. It would have taken away the sting. But he'd hoped for more, and now he was burning with anticipation.

"So, show me?" Dan asked.

"Follow me."

John led the way down the hall, into a lift. Dan wheeled himself along behind him, appreciating that his friend hadn't asked if he needed help with the chair. Independence was going to be a touchy subject for a while, and he was glad that John never even brought it up. The doors snapped shut after the two of them had entered, leaving the other crew from the shuttle unloading. The lift felt big with just the two of them; Dan noticed that John hadn't invited the other new arrivals, and no one else had come anywhere near this elevator.

He looked up at his old friend, saw new creases and lines that hadn't been there when they'd last met in person. The old sprinkling of gray had spread across his hair, too. It had been a couple of years, but it seemed like John had aged more than that.

Then John met his gaze. For a moment his face lit up with that boyish excitement again, before he schooled it back into a more serious mask. But the fire was still lit, there in his eyes if you knew him well enough to look. When John got that look, his enthusiasm was contagious.

The elevator was still descending. "Seems like we're going down a long way," Dan said.

"We are. The project is about half a kilometer below the surface."

"Why so deep? I thought you were mining helium?"

"We are, up top. This is another project. It's down deep because of security...and other reasons. You'll see. If you still want to be on board, after you hear the conditions." John pulled out a tablet computer from a deep leg pocket.

"First off, what you will be shown is a secret known to only about two dozen individuals, period. It can't go any farther than that. Not now, at least. I've gone to incredible lengths to ensure the tightest security possible for the project. If you want in, you have to agree to the terms beforehand. Two years here on the lunar base, no unmonitored contact with Earth allowed, no returns to Earth without my explicit permission. If you see the project and want out, that's fine; you'll be put up here at the base above us at my expense. No salary. If you sign on, you get the salary and benefits listed in the contract here."

He held the tablet out. Dan tried to read his mood as he took the device, but his friend had a good poker face on.

Dan scanned the contract and whistled. "I've

signed NDAs before, John. But the contract you're offering beats the Air Force all to hell."

John grinned down at him. "Well, that's the plus side of working in the private sector. And there's some hazard involved as well. You need to thumb-stamp the NDA now, but you can wait on the contract until you hear the details."

Dan pressed his thumb to the first document, tabbed to the second with his finger. He scanned the text. Two years at these rates would set him up for a long while to come, if he was careful with his cash. He shrugged and pressed his thumb into the stamp, letting the tablet take biometric readings and a fingerprint from him, sealing the contract. It wasn't like he had a lot of other plans.

"I trust you, John," he said, handing the tablet back. It was a big leap, but his gut said he wouldn't regret this.

The elevator shuddered to a stop, but the doors didn't open immediately. John pressed a thumb against a spot on the panel, and placed his eye before a retinal scanner. Only then did a light over the door glow green.

"Majel, allow access for myself plus one," John said.

The doors ground slowly open.

Dan was about to make a joke about John's ongoing affair with his computer, but what he saw stripped the thoughts from his mind. He rolled closer for a better look.

The room was enormous, but Dan didn't have eyes for the room. Instead, he was drawn to the centerpiece, a great latticework of aluminum scaffolding, gleaming softly in the light. And buried beneath the bars and beams, a ship.

At first glance, it looked a lot like the shuttle he had taken from the International Space Station to the moon. But where the lunar shuttles were blocky things, designed to fly in space, this looked aerodynamic. It had the sleek lines of a jet fighter, and delta shaped wings slipped gracefully from the sides of the ship. Sitting between the wings were the engines, which looked larger than anything Dan had seen on a shuttle before.

He waffled between curiosity and a sense of disappointment. The ship was gorgeous, but why all the secrecy over a new shuttle design? There had to be more to it. He glanced up at John, who merely shrugged and crossed his arms over his chest. He wanted Dan to figure out the mystery for himself? Fine, he could do that. He looked back at the ship, then began wheeling himself closer.

Dan rolled under the scaffolds in an arch-like spot, reaching out to touch the sleek metal. High density alloy composites – high grade stuff, horrifically expensive, he knew. The ship was built to take a beating, and to last for a long time. There were several doors down the side of the ship's twenty meter length, some open, some closed. A handful of men and women worked busily as bees around a hive, flitting here and there with components.

He rolled down toward the rear of the ship, intending to take a look at the engines. It didn't seem like the ship had a lot of space for fuel, so he had to wonder how much range it would have. Then he reached the engines, and stopped cold.

He'd expected to see the regular nozzles all rockets used to propel themselves with some combination of fuel and oxidizer. Mankind had been using that same system for primary propulsion for about a hundred years now.

This ship didn't have any nozzles. Or any sort of propulsion that he could discern. Instead, the rear of the ship was mounted with a series of large disks, each about the size of a tabletop. They seemed to be made of some sort of metal, but he couldn't identify the alloy on sight, and they were out of his reach.

As he examined them, his head started throbbing a little.

"Don't stare at them too long, Dan. The headaches are one bit we haven't figured out yet," John said. He'd walked in beside him while he was lost in examination.

"What do you mean, haven't figured out yet? Didn't you build them?"

"No. We found them. That's the secret."

"Found them?" Dan's brow furrowed. "Where?"

"Here, Dan. We found them here on the moon, half a kilometer below the surface. We discovered them when we found this cave. Along with a bunch of other things."

EIGHT

A hidden ship, buried on the moon? It wasn't possible. That was the stuff of science fiction, not reality. John had to be pulling his leg.

"You're messing with me. What's the story?" Dan asked.

"That's it," John said, shaking his head. His face was serious. "We almost missed the place entirely, because it was so deep. I was planning the solar and mining operation out here and sent probes over to look for underground caverns. It's easier and safer to convert underground spaces into living areas than to build domes on the surface. Healthier for the folks who have to live here, too. Anyway, one probe came back with an odd reading at this spot, so we went in for a closer look. At one point, this cave was part of some sort of larger complex. Mostly gone now, although we've unearthed a bit of it. But the hangar was intact, and there were the remains of a ship in here. An old, old ship."

"How old are we talking, John?" Dan asked quietly. He still felt like he ought to be waiting for the punchline of a joke.

"Maybe a thousand years. Maybe older. Hard to say for certain." He watched the corner of John's smile quirk up a little on his otherwise serious face.

The number floored him. A ship out here, a base out here, from a time before humanity had even learned about flight? Again, it didn't seem possible, but John wasn't wearing a joking face. Dan looked at the ship again, and the strange disks on the back immediately brought back his headache. They were strange, in a way he'd never seen before. Was this all for real?

"So you rebuilt the ship," he said. "What does the drive do? How does it work?"

"We haven't flown it yet. We have theories, but until we test, it's hard to say for sure. Not a lot of the ship survived, really, so it was a major rebuilding project. The power plant was intact, which was the most important component. The drives, too, which seem to be some sort of gravity drive. The main computer, although a lot of the database is either corrupted or beyond our ability to access. And a couple of other cool gadgets. Watch this," John said. Then he called out in a loud voice "Can we get a cloak demonstration, please?"

A couple of the crew nodded and bustled into the ship, heading toward the nose. Dan waited another minute, wondering what they were doing, and then the ship just vanished. One moment it was there, and the next it simply wasn't anymore. On instinct, Dan wheeled toward where the ship had been, but John reached out to stop him.

"Whoa! Not so fast, you'll hurt yourself. It's still there."

Dan braked, then reached out a tentative hand. He made contact with smooth metal, gliding under his fingers, completely unseen.

"It's invisible?"

"Yup." John had that kid's grin back in his voice, and looking over his shoulder Dan saw it was there on his face as well.

"Well, close to it anyway," he continued. "The cloak is actually a field. We think it was pre-set for the original size of the ship. It's not something we've been able to tinker with, anyway, so the field is still the same size. Over here, it matches the hull pretty completely, because we rebuilt the engine frame about the same. But up by the nose, there are patches you can stand inside the field and be as invisible as the ship."

Dan ran his hand over the invisible hull almost reverently, marveling at how solid and real it felt to his fingers, without even the slightest trace of its existence perceived by his eyes. "She's quite a ship, John. What do you have planned for her?"

"Well, I plan to take her up and go exploring. And I'd like you to fly her."

Dan closed his eyes and bowed his head a little, hand still resting on the hull. He was torn between profound awe and childlike wonder.

"You're one of the best, Dan. I need the best for this. Earth needs the best for this. You see – that drive on the back of the ship, while faster than anything else we have, is still just an in-system drive. The ship has a second drive as well."

Dan looked up, locked eyes with his friend.

"It's got a wormhole drive, too. Near as we can tell, anyway. It vanishes everything we send into it, and best we can extrapolate, it's shipping them someplace."

"You can't tell for sure?"

"The ship didn't really come with a manual," John replied with a wry grin. "We're figuring all this out as we go along, although we've made some headway in translating the language, thanks to Majel's assistance. The destinations programmed in all seem to be light years away. We sent out a couple of probes, but we think it might be decades before we get any kind of direct signal back from them. But when we opened the wormhole again we were able to make radio contact with the probes, and the video they sent back to us showed star-fields which were not from our solar system."

Dan settled back in his seat, trying to take it all in. "So you've found an impossible ship that's thousands of years old, buried in the moon. It can cloak. It can travel between stars. You intend to use it to go visiting these other stars. And you want me to fly her?" Dan watched John's smile grow wider with each word. As if there was any doubt how he would answer. "I am so in. Wouldn't miss it."

"Knew you'd be crazy enough that I could count on you."

There was a short buzzing sound, and the ship snapped back into view. The abrupt appearance of such a large object right in front of him was a startling experience for Dan. It was like it was not there one moment, and then suddenly visible.

"Who's messing about and slowing my work crews down?" asked a voice from nearer to the nose of the ship.

Dan blinked. He knew that voice. He pulled his wheelchair back to get a better look at the speaker.

And there she was, wearing the same bright orange jumpsuit as the other crew working on the ship. Her hair was back in a ponytail, but he knew if she pulled the hair tie out it would float about her head in a mass of uncontrollable brown curls. No makeup. She hardly ever wore any, and never when she was working. He'd never thought she needed it.

How long had it been?

Beth was taking long strides down the length of the ship toward them. Her mouth was set in a hard line, and her eyes narrowed a bit when she spared a quick glance for him.

"John," she said, "Bad enough you set me an impossible deadline. I don't need you down here mucking about and delaying my crew."

"Sorry," John said, the twinkle in his eye belying the contrite tone of voice. "I'll try to stay out of your way. I was just introducing Dan to the ship."

She looked down her nose at Dan. "Welcome aboard. I hope you can fly this thing as well as John thinks you can."

Dan felt his hackles raising at her tone. "I'm sure I can figure it out, if you and the grease monkeys can get her ready to fly."

John's eye movements flickered back and forth between them. "Right. OK, Dan, time to go. Lots to do. I've set you up in a room, and given you priority access to Majel's processor cycles, so she can work with you on simulations of piloting the ship. She's extrapolated the flight sim controls from the results of our experiments."

Beth had already turned and was walking back to her crew, calling out orders as she went, so Dan missed seeing her close her eyes, missed the pain etched in her brow. He only saw her stalk away from him.

He wheeled back to the lift, John following close behind. Dan waited until the lift doors had closed before saying another word.

"You could have warned me, John," Dan said, eyes locked on the elevator door.

"Would you have come, if I had? Or would you have kept drinking yourself into a stupor every night?"

"That's not fair." Dan spun in place to face John, one wheel going in each direction like the halves of his heart in that moment.

But it was probably an accurate assessment, he mused. The prospect of seeing Beth again might have been enough to keep him away.

"Do you regret coming?" John asked softly.

"No." The prospect of flying a ship to other stars? That trumped everything. It was every little kid's daydream. And a chance to live his adult dreams again, too. "No regrets."

NINE

C harline Foster pulled her van into a quiet alley nearby the Texatronic Industries headquarters building. She couldn't get onto the actual company campus anymore without raising too many eyebrows. Oh, she could probably hack a brief clearance for herself and be admitted. The guys working the main gate knew her. They wouldn't think anything was up if she popped in one more time to grab a few things.

But then she'd be on cameras. Her arrival and departure times would be logged. Charline wanted this little expedition to be so totally off the books that no one would be able to trace any of it back to her. So instead of slipping into the compound, her van was parked half a mile away, between Terry's Bar and a store covered with signs saying they would 'pay top dollar' for gold and silver. It wasn't the sort of neighborhood she wanted to stay in for long, but it ought to be OK for long enough to get the job done.

She glared down at her laptop as she hammered the keys. Fire her, would they? Charline fumed quietly to herself. She was the one who Fred Heimsman had come on to. She was the one he'd asked into his office for a private conference, which turned into a session of him asking her for a 'special massage'. Which she declined, and when the asshole tried to persist she hammered the point home with her knee into his groin.

Charline had taken the issue directly to Human Resources. She'd been told to go home, that they would deal with the matter. Three days later she was holding a pink slip. Was that really how they thought the world worked? They figured they could just get rid of the victim and absolve themselves of problems? Charline had already contacted a lawyer who was going to have a little chat with them later in the day.

But first, she was going to get a little of her own back. They'd hired Charline because she was one of the best network defense specialists in the world.

Well, they were about to learn that all of those tricks that made her good at securing their systems could also be used for an offensive.

The night before, she'd piloted a small drone onto their campus. The tiny thing was only a little bigger than her hand. So small that it was hard to hear, and almost impossible to spot the dark gray body at night. The drone was carrying a wifi extender, along with all the protocols it needed to link into the main building's wireless internet. With the extender, Charline didn't need to be in the building to access their secure internal network. She could punch directly into their hardware from right where she was.

The first computer she went into was Heimsman's. She was curious how he'd managed to avoid getting the boot. Why had they dumped her instead? It became obvious pretty quickly. Heimsman had some potent blackmail material. Seems the company CEO had been involved in some extra-curricular activities while on a company retreat. Things that the Board of Directors - and his wife - would likely be a little upset about. Charline grabbed the files and set them to upload to Heimsman and the CEO's public Facebook accounts in an hour. That ought to make life interesting for them.

It also meant that she was on a clock. Someone would notice the Facebook posts within minutes of when they went live. It wouldn't take them long to realize their security had been breached. Charline had about an hour to do the rest of her damage.

The job took her half of that.

She hammered the system with everything she had. Her hand-crafted virus tore through their storage, reducing saved files to gibberish. Along the way she found a bunch of other files which were incriminating in one way or another. Those she grabbed and stored on her laptop. It might be useful at some point to have a little leverage - you never knew when it might come in handy to be able to threaten a few key people with prison time.

Then she smoked the machines themselves. Charline figured she was bricking a few tens of millions of dollars in hardware. By the time she was halfway through, the security teams inside the building had started to catch on. They were trying to take the network offline to protect what hadn't been hit yet, but it was way too late for that. She'd trained half of those people. It wasn't hard to hack circles around them.

Oh, the company would survive. But between the data loss and the dead servers, she'd cost them about as much as her salary would have been for the next forty years. Served them right. Charline carefully disconnected from the servers, covering her tracks with each step of her retreat. Not that there was much left of the machines she'd invaded, but she wasn't taking any chances. Then she pressed a button which would order the drone to fly out into the Gulf of Mexico and drown itself in the ocean.

Leaning back in her seat, she stared down at the laptop. It was done. She'd finished the job. Why didn't she feel much better, then? The bad guys had got theirs. It just wasn't enough to wash away the slimy feeling that lingered from the assault, and the even worse one from being fired for reporting it. Charline heaved a deep sigh and set the computer aside. It was time to move on, physically as well as emotionally. With her skills she shouldn't have too hard a time finding a new job.

Someone rapped on the side door of her van.

Charline only froze in place for a second. Then her hand went to the small pistol in her purse. She pulled out the gun. Her parents hadn't raised a fool. It never hurt to be cautious. She shot a glance at the side view mirror. There was only one guy outside. He had short-cropped sandy hair that was a little darker than her blonde. He was athletically built, wearing a dark suit and a tie. Was he a cop? The haircut and build screamed military or law enforcement. His outfit looked more corporate than federal employee, but it was hard to tell for sure sometimes. She aimed the pistol out toward the man and opened the side door of the van a few inches.

"What do you want? Am I blocking something?" Charline asked him.

His smile warmed the man's face up considerably. "No, I'm just looking for someone. Are you a Ms. Charline Foster?"

"Who's asking?"

"My name is Andy Wakefield. I understand you were recently fired?" he asked.

What was this about? Why was he asking about her job? What was this guy up to? "Maybe. You hiring?"

"Not me, but as a matter of fact, my employer wants to bring you on board for a special project," Andy said.

"Wait - you're offering me a job?" Charline said.

"Yup."

Charline thought about it a few seconds. She had a lot of cash saved up. More than anything else, what she needed was some time. Take a trip, go on vacation, see some of the world. Her skills would be as viable in a couple of months as they were now, and taking some time for herself sounded more fun. Plus, who was going to seriously trust random men making job offers in dark alleys? The thing stank.

"How did you find me?" she asked, stalling and hoping for a little more information. Her hand remained tight around her pistol.

"License plate. Got it from the local camera systems. I knew you were in the neighborhood, so I looked around. Not a lot of vans out here," he said.

Shit. She'd forgotten the traffic camera systems. That data would put her darned close to the hack at the time it went down. It wasn't directly incriminating, but it was a potential problem. Maybe it was time to take that vacation after all. Ideally someplace far away. How had this guy managed to access traffic cam data so quickly, anyway? Was he a hacker too? Charline felt a little spike of curiosity, but clamped down on it. She wasn't about to go out like the proverbial cat.

"No, thanks. Think I'm all set," she said, slamming the door shut. He didn't try to stop her, and she heaved a sigh of relief. Quickly she slid up into the driver's seat and stuck her key in the ignition.

"All right," he said from outside. "But if you change your mind and want to come work on a quantum computer system anytime in the next forty-eight hours, give me a call."

Wait. Quantum what? There were a few people messing around with some quantum chips, but no one had an actual computer running yet. Did they?

"You're mixing me with someone else. I don't do tech development. I'm a software girl, not hardware," she hollered out at him. She twisted the key and the van coughed to life.

"This isn't hardware development," he said.

Charline turned off the van. If they were looking for someone to develop software for a quantum computer, this wasn't just bleeding edge - it was damned near science fiction. No one had that sort of tech yet. At least, no one she'd ever heard about. Which meant that this deal was something so far off the books that there wasn't even a whisper of it out there. If there was, she'd have heard it. Her curiosity burned brighter than ever, and with a groan, she gave in to temptation. This Andy had known precisely what to say to get her attention.

She leaned over the passenger's seat and opened the door. "Get in. No funny business. I have a pistol and I know how to shoot it."

"No worries. I'm here to hire you, not to bother you. If you want me to get out anytime while we talk, just stop the van and I'll leave. You won't hear from me again," Andy said to her as he got in and sat down.

Charline started the van up again, burning with questions she wanted to ask. She had the feeling she wasn't going to ask the guy to leave.

TEN

The next few days flew by. John watched all the moving parts as carefully as he could, trying to make sure he didn't drop the ball on anything. It was exhausting work, not made easier by the fact that he was also managing a legitimate business. The mining work was critical to the Earth. The US military had first dibs on his helium-3, but he had governments – multiples – bargaining with him for output, once the mining operation was completely operational. For now, it was only producing a trickle supply. But the desperation in those negotiations disturbed him. It meant the energy situation was far worse than the public media was broadcasting, and the public version was bad enough.

And in his experience desperate governments take desperate actions. The last thing he wanted was for some government to decide they ought to control his operations up here. It could spark a war over the moon, if one government tried to claim the helium-3 resources here. That fighting over essential energy would lead to mass power outages on Earth was the least of the trouble. Without power, farms would fail. Transportation would break down. Starvation, looting, a breakdown of civil services - the result of a war could be catastrophic worldwide. Worse yet if that war resulted in discovery of the ship. Because it had the power to solve the problem, which would instead make everything worse.

The ship's engine drew power from an enormous power source that they still didn't understand. None of his people had been able to determine precisely what its power output limits were, or how long it would last. They didn't even have a good working theory about how it operated. But the ship used more power to hold a wormhole open for a few seconds than the entire North American continent.

For a planet that was tottering on the brink of energy collapse, it would be a panacea. If he could reveal that it existed at all. Because the energy crisis also had all the major powers, from China, to the USA, to the EU, to India, on the verge of war. All it would take would be a spark.

A spark like a single device that would solve all the energy issues, for whomever controlled it. A device that was based on such an alien technology that it would be decades, if ever, before humans could replicate it and build other such devices. Whoever controlled the ship's power supply would have the entire world in the palm of their hand. No nation would allow any other to keep it.

No, revealing the ship was out of the question. It would ignite a bloodbath such as the planet had never seen.

The lift he was riding settled to a stop a level above the hangar. That floor was living and working space for the project's crew. The elevator chimed, breaking him from his reverie. A quick retinal scan, and the doors opened for him. He had called for a staff meeting of all the principals involved. They'd be the crew for the first mission. And he still intended to fly the ship the day after tomorrow, if all went well.

The doors to the meeting room opened in front of him. Several team members were already present and seated around a table. Beth was arguing with her second engineer, Paul Weston. Dan was reading something on a tablet, studiously ignoring the pair of them. That the two engineers were arguing wasn't especially unusual. But since neither of them noticed him come in, John stood to listen to their debate.

"...and I still think it's too risky, Beth. We've been lucky so far, but we ought to be bringing the government into this now. It's too big. Too important," Paul said.

"But what would they do with her, Paul?" she asked. "Hide her somewhere? Pick her apart like a carcass? After all the work we did to restore her?"

"What's the problem?" John asked, announcing his presence.

"Paul thinks we ought to hand the ship over to the government," Beth said. "I hate the idea."

"We haven't needed them so far," Paul replied. "We've done great things. But don't we have a responsibility to share this?"

Paul looked around the room. "Listen, I know this is a touchy subject, but we all know how important – how powerful an asset – this ship is. When people find out about it – and they will find out, sooner or later – there's going to be hell to pay."

Interesting that they seemed to be discussing the same thing which had been on his mind a minute before. Then again, maybe it was inevitable that his decision to keep the ship a secret would be questioned. John was glad Beth was still on his side regarding the matter. He wasn't sure what he would do if both engineers presented a united front against him.

"And if we hand it to the US government, and word leaks out to other countries, Paul? What then?" asked John.

Paul opened his mouth to reply, then closed it. He looked down at the table, his cheeks flushing with anger.

"The ship is simply too powerful. The other nations of the world would never let it stand. It would be war," John said.

"At least it would be a war our side would win," Paul said, tension and pride in his voice.

"Nobody wins that kind of war," Dan said, looking up from his tablet for the first time to lock eyes with Paul. Paul broke away first.

"We go ahead as planned. At least for now," John said. "You OK with that, Paul?"

Paul grimaced, then nodded. John watched him for a little longer. He was going to have to keep an eye on the man. Paul wasn't just suggesting the idea. He seemed to be angry at being told no. Paul was rash enough to perhaps take action even after he'd been denied. John made a mental note to have Majel keep an eye on him. It would be difficult for him to communicate to Earth without John knowing about it, but not impossible even with all the security he had in place. There were too many people coming and going on the upper levels, delivering supplies and taking helium-3 back to Earth. The mine was a great disguise for the other operations on the base, but it also represented their biggest security hole.

"OK. Let's get down to our main business, shall we? Beth, what's the state of the ship?" John asked.

"The ship could use another month or two, John. You know that. I told you the same thing yesterday."

"Yes, I know, Beth. I also know engineers would always like another month or two." John grinned. "Will she fly, day after tomorrow?"

Beth sighed and said "Yes. She'll be ready to fly."

"Excellent. Now, Majel is the only AI we've got

available, and we don't have the hardware to clone her here. How long will it take to transfer her over?"

"I can answer that," said a woman's voice from the doorway behind him.

This time it had been John's turn to miss the doors slipping open. He looked over his shoulder and caught a glimpse of Andrew leading in a young woman he assumed was the latest acquisition for their team. Beth had the mechanical and electrical engineering down cold. But the ship had an alien computer system which they had made communicate with human-built computers to control it. It had taken a great effort to make that work, more than John liked, and he wanted an expert on hand to help smooth the process some as they went forward. He glanced down at his tablet, tapping it to open her file. The photo was the same. This was Charline Foster.

"Ah, our computer genius! I'm delighted you decided to join us. Thanks for coming up here to help with this." John took his own seat, as Charline stepped into the room.

Dan perked up at seeing her escort. "Andy! Good to see you again! Didn't know you'd be joining us."

"Andrew is my one man security detail for this trip, Dan," said John.

"Security, eh? A man of many talents," Dan said. Winking at Andrew, he grasped the chair next to him and pulled it out from the table a bit. Andrew accepted with a nod and sat next to him.

"Good," John said. "Charline is one of the best interface programmers in the world. She's here to help us get Majel installed into the systems, and help us get the human control components working properly with the original ones. I know you've got it running," he held up a hand toward Beth to forestall protest. "She'll help hammer out any rough spots."

"Wasn't going to argue," Beth said. She offered Charline a genuine smile. "That's not my specialty, and we could certainly use the help."

"I'm thinking that the actual AI interface shouldn't take that long, provided all we're doing is creating a basic load from the base computer to the ones we installed on the ship," Charline said.

"How long?" John asked.

"A few hours for the install. A few more to test. Call it a full day of work, just in case there are some snags, and then let Majel get settled in running diagnostics overnight."

"Well, you know what you're doing tomorrow, I guess," Dan said.

She nodded. Conversation wound around other unfinished issues, most of them minor. John realized he'd set a brutal pace to get the rebuild completed on this timeline, but now everything was almost complete. The ship was almost ready. He just couldn't help feeling that the clock was ticking. Paul was right on one count; he wasn't going to be able to hide this forever, and as soon as the secret got out, every government in the world would be vying to wrest the ship out of his hands.

"OK," John said finally, "Something else, which some of you already know and some of you don't. The ship was damaged when we found it. Not just the damage of years of sitting there, but scarring and pitting. We subjected the damaged bits to tests and microscopic analysis, and came to the conclusion that they were impacted by some sort of high-energy discharge."

"Ray guns," Dan supplied incredulously. "Someone shot the ship down?"

"No, none of the damage was critical. But there were signs that the base itself might have been under some sort of attack. Hard to say; the damage was very old, but it looked like more of the same."

"Which is why I'm here, at least in part," Andrew said, relaxing back into his chair.

"Yes. Andrew is a...lot of things. But among them, he's a weapons specialist. And we're mounting a pair of guns on the wings of the ship – railgun cannons, basically," John said. The guns would fire magnetized hunks of metal down their tubes. There had been some use of magnetic guns on Earth before, but not much. The limit was always the power available. Tying the guns into the ship's main power plant had solved that issue quickly. The ship had unbelievable amounts of power to spare.

John went on quickly. "The point is, this ship had probably seen battle, all those years ago. We don't know who it was fighting for, or against. We don't know who won, or even if whomever it was is still out there. But we know that there are beings out there who were capable of making weapons of great power back when humans were first learning about building cities. We don't know what we might face, but we'll be as prepared as we can be."

"This first flight, though, is just a quick up and about. We'll time it for when those pesky satellites are as far away as possible, turn on the cloak, fly up, and put her through her paces here in the system," Beth said. She stared meaningfully at Dan. "Nothing fancy."

Dan shrugged with a small grin, as if to say 'who, me'?

"Any questions?" John asked.

There were none. John dismissed the crew, and they practically bounced out of the room, some of them chatting with each other, off to finish what still needed doing. He stayed behind, staring at his tablet, wondering again what problems he might have missed. And wondering how long humanity had before it came across the original owners of this ship, or whatever it was that had shot at her.

ELEVEN

I t was night shift on the base. The lights were dimmed in the ship hangar, casting a low light in a pool around the ship. While they could in theory draw power for the base from the ship's engine, John had never set things up that way. He wanted the ship and base to be independent from one another. The base ran off mostly solar energy, with a backup generator inside. As a result, conserving power was still the norm.

The AI for the facility, designated Majel by its owner, detected movement coming down the ladder from the crew section above the hangar. The computer activated its cameras in the room with some difficulty. The new computer aboard the ship was still connected to the base computer by a hard line of thick cable, but the result was the AI's attention was split between the two systems. To make things worse, it was tracking hundreds of cameras, dozens of objects in space around Luna, and its user had put priority on running diagnostics on the new systems to which it had been attached.

Majel wasn't a true artificial intelligence; she was a very powerful computer program, however, able to perform massive multitasking with ease. She was even programmed with some limited ability to predict system demands and prepare to allocate resources for those anticipated tasks. She still needed direction to act, however. And over the last twenty four hours, she'd been given an overabundance of directions.

Her processors housed enormous computational abilities. And they were under strain.

So when her cameras picked up an orange suited man entering the hangar wearing a tool belt, her program routed a few CPU cycles to verify that he was indeed staff (scanning his face for recognition). Another few cycles indicated that he was indeed a tech, did indeed use tools here on a daily basis, and had in fact been in the hangar earlier that day. The program took moments to recognize this data, and conclude that his presence was acceptable. That given, it shut down direct monitoring of the cameras, putting those CPU cycles back into use for the diagnostics checks.

Which meant that no one, not even the computer guardian, was paying attention as the man opened the ship's main hatch and stepped inside. No one was there to notice as he made his way through the main corridor to the engine compartment. No one observed him removing several panels and making adjustments to the systems within.

Once he was done, he quietly replaced the panels. He set every one back precisely as it had been. This operation had been planned out for weeks now. Even though John's accelerated timetable had forced him to push himself to the limit to get everything in place, it was going smoothly so far. Everything was perfect. In a short time, the starship would be in safer hands, under the control of people who could use it responsibly. He'd worked hard for this day.

It was none too soon. Not that he didn't trust John. Quite the contrary. He felt like his boss was an exceptional man, and the work he was doing was incredible. But he was taking too many risks. No one person ought to be making the decisions he was by himself. They had a ship which was capable of reaching other stars - stars they already knew had other life residing on them somewhere. The outer hull of the original alien ship, pitted and scarred by what certainly looked like energy weapon impacts, was evidence enough that those other beings were a lot like humans. They were capable of war, of killing, of brutal military action.

John planned to take the ship out exploring, which was the childhood dream of everyone who'd ever thought about going into space. But it was too great a chance to take. They might well attract attention of the wrong kind out there. They could wind up bringing enemies back to Earth, against which the planet was poorly defended. He saw disaster looming down that road.

Or they could turn the ship over to the government. With some work, the power source could be used to give cheap energy to the entire United States. If someone else wanted it? Let them come try and take it. He felt confident that his nation would be able to secure and hold the ship once it was turned in. Then they could have the best minds in the world learning from the ancient vessel. In time they could replicate its technologies and build other engines like it. Then they could go exploring -

not with one ship, but with an armada of vessels capable of taking on whatever they ran into.

It wouldn't hurt that he would be hailed as a hero for being the one to do the right thing, but that wasn't his primary motive.

Once the compartment was back the way it had been, he pulled four small black cylinders from his tool belt. They looked like regular bolts, but each was packed with a potent explosive. The first of these he set in the engine room, careful to place it far from the irreplaceable alien components. A quick hole drilled in the deck, and the bolt was inserted. It looked like a hundred other bolts around the room. The second, he installed in the bridge.

Then he stepped back outside the ship, closing the hatch. He walked around underneath the ship's belly, gleaming softly by the glow of a dim flashlight. Toward the rear of the ship, he drilled two new holes and inserted the bolts, locking them in place with sealant to prevent air leaks. No one would notice the little additions he'd made. The bombs were carefully crafted to look like they belonged on the ship. When the flight crews went over the vessel to look for pre-flight problems in the morning, everything would look as it ought to.

Everything was ready now. Soundless, he

crossed the room to the ladder, avoiding the lift. No sense risking running into someone now. Not with everything going according to plan. Tomorrow he would leave with the crew, disable the ship, and turn it over to the government. Tomorrow he'd be the most famous name on the planet, a hero who's face would be remembered as the man who'd done the right thing even when it was supremely difficult.

TWELVE

Dan woke before his alarm, his head already buzzing with excitement. He rolled to a sitting position on the edge of his bed and grasped the sides of the walker in front of him. With a grunt, he pushed himself up from the bed. His legs didn't give him a lot of support, but the rehab had paid off a little. The limbs had just enough strength to keep him upright each time he moved the walker forward. In Earth's gravity, the whole thing probably would have been impossible. But on Luna he only weighed about thirty pounds. His legs could keep that up for the second it took to push the walker a bit.

He grunted again and took another step. And another. His doc at the med center would probably have kittens if he saw Dan now. He was talking about getting Dan fitted out for a lower body exoskeleton, motors and gears all reactive to the slightest twitch he made. He'd read about them before, a civilian version of the LEGs – Light Exoskeleton Garment, he figured the Army was to blame for that acronym – infantry wore into combat these days.

Maybe it would work. Maybe not. But he'd been figuring out what he was capable of himself, these days. After spending so many months just giving in to sloth in the chair, it felt...right.

Another hard push. He tottered a bit, and almost fell. Caught his balance in time.

And then he was there, positioning the walker just so...

A sigh of relief.

The toilet was a real basin but not filled with water. Lower gravity has a way of making every-thing feel different. Even taking a pee. He hit the flush button, and a bit of chemical goop scoured the sides of the toilet, suction washing the whole mess out into a pipe. It reminded him of the toilet in an airplane.

Then he turned the walker around and started the slow walk back to the bed so he could get ready for the day. This was the big day, after all. He was going to be a space pilot again. But even that satisfaction paled a bit against the simple pleasure of being able to take care of himself again.

Such a small thing, going to the bathroom. Something he'd taken for granted his entire life. But after months of getting around by wheelchair, just being able to do that simple task felt like a massive accomplishment. And the first of many for today. He tried to keep his hands from shaking as he put on a dark gray flight suit. Today, he'd be flying the wildest experimental vehicle in the history of mankind.

A short while later he was set. He grabbed his tablet and slid it into a leg pocket, slapping the velcro tab closed. A quick shift into his wheelchair, and he was off. Down the hall, into the lift, and off to the adventure.

Who cared about Mars, anyway?

The lift doors opened into the hangar, and a buzz of activity. He watched as techs ran down their checklists. He'd seen the pre-flight checks. The document was about fifty pages long, and it seemed like overkill to him. But anything not working right could be deadly, so he appreciated the meticulous attention to detail the guys in orange displayed.

They were going over the ship with the proverbial fine-toothed comb, looking for anything which might cause problems. Beth had sworn to scrub the mission if anything came up. From the look on her face, nothing had. She wasn't happy about taking the ship out so soon. Dan hoped John was making the right call. Whatever else he might think about Beth, she was terrific at her job.

John was already by the nose of the ship, dressed in a flight suit and holding a large bottle of champagne in his hand. He looked like a kid on Christmas morning. There was so much energy built up inside him that Dan was surprised he wasn't hopping from one foot to the other in anticipation.

Dan wheeled over to say hello. "Morning, John. What did you decide to name her, anyway? You never told me."

"He never told anyone," Beth said, rolling her eyes.

"I'm keeping it a surprise," John replied.

Dan cocked an eyebrow. "You're not naming it..."

"No, not what you're thinking," John said with a laugh.

Dan shrugged. "Can't help a guy for wondering.

You did name your AI Majel, after all. It's not too big a jump from that to naming your starship after the Enterprise."

Dan heard the lift open again, and looked over. That was Andy and Charline coming in, which rounded off the crew. Those two, himself, Beth, Paul, and John. Paul and Beth had been against John coming a couple of days ago, arguing that he should stay on the moon and play mission control, at least for this first test flight. But John would have none of it. This was his baby, and he wanted to go. Honestly, Dan couldn't really blame him. Not after watching the Mars mission take off without him. He never wanted to make anyone feel like that.

So John was in. As mission commander. Fair – he'd worked as hard as anyone at making this day a reality. Harder than most.

The techs seemed to have finished the last of their checks, and were reporting in to Paul with their results. Paul looked over at John and gave a thumbs-up sign.

"Looks like we're on," John said.

He motioned for everyone to gather around the nose of the starship.

"I wanted to thank all of you," he said, bowing

his head a little and speaking softly enough that people had to crane in to hear him.

Then he looked up at the people gathered around him. "You've worked hard, very hard. You've done something amazing, something most folks would have probably thought impossible. You've taken an ancient, dead craft from the stars, and you've made it ours."

"Ours. Yours. Mine. Humanity's."

"That word ought to mean something special to all of us, today. We all know now that humanity is not alone in the universe. We might have thought that we were not alone, before. Hoped for it. Feared it. But all of us here today know the truth – there really are aliens on other worlds. And if there's one race out there other than ours, there are probably more. Maybe hundreds of others, out there among the stars," John said.

He beckoned toward the ceiling, fingers outstretched like he could grasp those bright lights through the rock over their heads.

His voice dropped to almost a whisper. "Today, we join them."

John took two steps closer to the ship, then reached out to lay a hand on it. The touch was gentle, careful, like a caress. All of the emotions

John was feeling were evident in that simple stroke of a hull panel. Dan could feel the excitement in the room, and the passion.

"Today," John said, gaining volume as he spoke, "we take our first steps toward the stars. Today, we leave behind what we were and reach for what we can be! And so – today, ladies and gentlemen –"

John raised the bottle high above his head. Then with a sharp motion, he smashed it over the nose of the ship.

"I give you the *Satori!*" John's voice had reached a baritone crescendo. And suddenly, everything clicked for Dan.

Satori had been an amazing woman. Her death had almost broken John.

Space had been her dream. She'd wanted to reach out and touch the stars.

And now, John had found a way to bring her there.

Dan found himself cheering with everyone else, and crying at the same time. He looked around and saw flushed faces and bright eyes. None of them would forget this moment. John caught his glance, cocked his head at an angle. Dan bowed his head, smiled.

"It was the right name, John," he said softly.

John closed his eyes. "She's the only star in my sky, you know."

Dan nodded in understanding. Then the emotional moment passed, and John was all business again.

"All right everyone. Places. Crew aboard, everyone else to the flight control room," John said. "Liftoff in fifteen minutes."

THIRTEEN

A ndrew watched Dan snap the latches that clicked his chair into place on the deck of the bridge. He smiled in admiration. John had been right about him, that was for sure. He'd been a wreck when Andy picked him up outside that bar. He honestly wasn't sure what Dan would be like once he had cleaned himself up and dried out a bit. But the man who wheeled himself up the ship's ramp and settled himself down in front of the flight controls was a completely different person from the broken shell Andy had first seen. Dan had been through the wringer, but he was every inch the professional in here. A man completely in his element.

Andy looked around the control room. Six

seats, six consoles. Dan's console faced forward, toward the curved window at the front of the ship. An empty seat was next to him, also facing the front – that would be Paul's, but he was in the engine room. They had two engineers on the trip, so one would remain back with the alien engine and power systems to monitor them while the other rode in the front of the ship. Keeping the engineers separate meant they could handle any problems on either end. More darkly, if something catastrophic happened and one of them was hurt or killed, the remaining engineer might still be able to do something from the other compartment.

Four more seats were along the outer walls, two per side. Each had a console. Technically, anyone could do their job from any console. Only Dan's was specially built with controls for steering the ship through space, but even that could be managed from one of the other stations in a pinch. Again, redundancy on everything they could manage was at the core of the ship's design.

Everyone else was taking their seats at consoles. He slipped into his own, near the back of the bridge. Not for the first time, Andy wondered what the heck he was doing here. He was present as a weapons specialist, sure. But he was more of a field man, not a desk jockey. He'd practiced working with the railgun controls enough that he could operate them like a pro. The worried voice in the back of his head had a funny feeling that anyone they ran into capable of achieving star-flight was going to laugh off the iron shells his weapons spat out. Any fight they got into would be short indeed.

"Control, evacuate air from the hangar," John said from the seat next to him.

Red lights flashed outside the ship as huge pumps prepared to pull the air from the room. Andrew felt himself holding his breath, and had to stop himself. The ship had its own atmosphere. If their seals failed, this was going to be one of the shortest space missions ever, and holding his breath wasn't going to help.

"Bring drives on line, Beth," John said.

"Drives on line...now," she replied.

There was a collective grunt as the engines lifted the ship off its landing struts a few inches and everyone's weight more than doubled in an instant. The drive created a gravity field within the ship, but it wasn't Earth normal gravity. Whatever planet the ship's builders had been from, they seemed to be comfortable in about three quarters the gravity of

Earth. Still, after the gentle gravity of Luna, even three quarters felt briefly uncomfortable.

"Helm responsive," Dan said.

"Control, open bay doors," John said into his radio.

"Door bays opening," came the response from the flight control room. "Godspeed, *Satori*."

Huge doors opened on one side of the hangar, revealing an upward-bending tunnel. It had been there when the humans arrived, a remnant element of the ancient base. John had crews clear rubble and reinforce the tunnel, but it had been largely intact. It opened on the surface, some miles away from the lunar base he'd built, and it was their passage into space.

"Dan, bring us out," John said. Andrew found himself holding his breath again as the ship slipped forward toward the exit. But Dan was as good as John said, it seemed. He eased the ship out of the hangar and into the tunnel, then adjusted the angle of the ship slightly, tilting up toward the surface, and applied more power.

The front of the bridge was a set of huge transparent panels, windows to see out into the world. Ahead – it was hard for Andrew to think about it as up, because of the gravity field – he could see stars.

He gripped the arms of his chair hard as the ship leapt toward that starfield. Rock flashed past the windows.

"Easy Dan," said John. "Keep it gentle. This is our first run."

Dan nodded, and the speed tapered off a bit. The ship flew steady as an arrow. And then they were out in open space, flying free of the moon. Dan accelerated a little more once they were free of the tunnel, and the lunar surface dropped away beneath them.

Before Andy could exhale the breath he hadn't realized he'd been holding, the radio crackled. "*Satori*, this is Control. We've picked up a course change from one of those satellites. They must have noticed something – they're headed your way."

"Andrew?" John asked.

"Confirmed, John. Getting the telemetry on the satellite from Control now. They're over the horizon still, so no line of sight, but it looks like they're making a bee-line for us."

"Time to go into sneaky mode, I think," said John. "They'll wonder where we went, but I don't think they'll assume the ship suddenly turned invisible. I wonder what they saw that made them head over this way, though? That could be important."

Beth pressed some keys on her console, frowned, and tried the sequence again. Her brow furrowed, and she tapped a few more keys. "I'm not getting any response from the cloak," she said.

"Bad time for that to break! Can we abort and return to base?" John asked.

"No time. They'll see us before we can get tucked inside," Dan replied.

"All right. Dan, keep us low to the moon, moving away from the satellite. Try to keep us under the horizon from them," John said.

Dan's hands moved deftly over his console, and Andy felt the ship alter course in response. His view of the moon spun wildly in the windows, but he could barely feel the change in course. Something about the way the engines worked was supposed to block or reduce the inertia they felt from course changes. Andy guessed at least that tech was working. Which was a good thing, because they would have pulled some serious Gs in that turn otherwise. John stepped up from his chair and went over to Beth's console to see what was going on.

"Paul, can you see if there's something interfering with the cloak? It's not responding to my controls here, maybe you can activate it from the engine room?" Beth said into the intercom. No response. "Paul?"

A warning burst of intuition tingled up the back of Andy's neck, that little signal that had kept him alive in dozens of hot situations over his life. Something was wrong. The satellite knowing to change course. The cloak conveniently not working precisely when they needed it most. Paul suddenly not answering from the engine room. Something was up. Something bad. He started to turn away from his console display.

Then a flash of intense pain exploded in Andy's skull, and he slipped away into unconsciousness.

FOURTEEN

T he crack of metal on bone drew the eyes of everyone on the bridge. John looked over to see what was up, sparing just a quick glance before bringing his attention back to the screen tracking that blasted satellite. Then he realized what he had seen, looked back again, and stared.

Everyone else was staring, too. Having a pistol aimed in one's general direction was a decidedly uncomfortable feeling. The weapon Paul held was small, but the diameter of a muzzle isn't all the relevant when it's being pointed in your direction.

"Paul, what the hell are you doing?" Beth asked, her eyes wide.

Andy was slumped over in his harness, blood

trickling from a spot just behind his ear. Paul stood next to him, a pistol in hand. His grip on the gun looked very steady. His lips were a thin, determined line, but a sheen of sweat showed on his forehead.

"I'm taking the ship, Beth. Doing what we all should have done," Paul replied.

"You traitor," John said, his face pale.

Paul trained the gun directly on John. "I'm not the traitor. I'm not the one who'd deny the most powerful weapon ever discovered to his country. Who'd keep it to himself like a new toy. I am a patriot, John."

Dan was still mostly focused on flying the ship. They were too close to the moon for him to be distracted long. John could see the telemetry Control was sending them projected on the main screen. Another satellite up ahead had changed course to cut them off. They were stuck between two of the things, and it wouldn't be long before one or both satellites got close enough to see them.

"John, we've got maybe two minutes before they're able to get visual imagery of the ship," Dan said, confirming his fears.

John nodded. He had two minutes. Had to keep calm if this was to come out right. Above all else he was not willing to put this ship into the hands Paul had in mind. Even if it was the US government, that was bad enough. Word would leak out, and war for the ship would become almost inevitable. But there was no guarantee that just because Paul thought he was working with the United States that he actually was. John had put out feelers into the US intelligence community, listening as carefully as he could for any word about leaks. He might have missed one. It was possible. But he was fairly sure that the US hadn't discovered the ship yet.

"What do you want, Paul?" John asked.

"Simple, really. Just hold course. The satellite ahead of us isn't unmanned; it has a crew of marines on board. They've got small craft that they'll use to jet over here, I'll let them into the ship, and we fly back to Earth."

"And if we refuse?" John asked.

If John was right about his guess, there might well be men over there ready to take his ship. But the troops probably weren't from the US military. Whether they represented some smaller nation or a corporate interest he didn't know, but based on the intelligence he had, it was unlikely to be US soldiers. Bad as war over the Satori would be if the United States obtained it, he couldn't imagine the danger if someone else won the ship. Imagine the ability to strike from a ship that could make itself invisible. No, better that the ship be destroyed than fall into nefarious hands. John thought hard, hoping to find some way out of this which didn't end with all of them dead.

"Then I start shooting people, John," Paul said. The deadpan way he said it sent chills down John's spine.

"A minute and thirty," Dan called out. "I can't evade both satellites unless we break away from the moon, and then they'll see us for sure."

John clenched and unclenched his hands. "Paul, think about this. Please – if we bring the ship back to Earth, if we give it to a government, any government... The other governments would never allow it. Never allow one nation to have that sort of power. It would be war."

"We aren't going to bring the ship back. I am," Paul said. "You lot will be going to jail for treason. Now, cuff yourselves with these," he said, tossing zip ties to John, Beth, and Charline.

"None for me?" Dan asked.

"I don't know how to fly the ship. Besides, it's not like you're going to rush me in that wheelchair, right? Do anything I don't like, and I start shooting your friends here."

John moved his gaze to each of his crew. When his eyes met Beth's, he saw her jaw set in a determined line. He knew that look – she was about to try something. He gave her a little head shake. Barely noticeable, but she caught it. He saw the desperation leave her eyes a little. She was counting on him to come up with something to get them out of this mess.

Now if only he could do something that would actually save them.

"You can't have her, Paul," John said. He worked to keep his tone even, despite the rage growing inside him. This man wanted to take his ship, steal *Satori* from him? He let a feral smile leak onto his face.

Paul saw and stalked closer to him, which is what he wanted.

"Cuff yourself, John. Now, or I shoot someone."

John snapped the zip ties around his wrists. He needed Paul to be a little closer.

"You coward," he spat.

That did the trick. Paul's face reddened, and he stepped close enough to punch John once, in the gut. John had braced for the blow, but the air whooshed out of his lungs and he almost fell over.

But that was enough. Paul was close to him now, which meant his attention wasn't on Dan anymore. As Paul raised his hand to hit him again, John gathered in a deep breath.

"Dan – ad astra!" John said.

DAN HEARD THE ORDER. Ad astra. It was Latin, and meant 'to the stars'. It was a toast the two of them had shared back in college, when they first stepped onto the roads which would lead them into space. It had been John's idea to use the toast as a code word now.

Dan didn't even take a deep breath before executing the order. He'd practiced this with Majel enough times in the simulator – not the part about having a gunman in the bridge, but if that order was ever given, it would be a true crisis. It was a desperate move that might kill all of them, but he'd known the risks when he signed on for this job. He hadn't been expecting to stare death in the face quite so soon, but every space flight had danger.

Dan checked the screen as he entered a code on his console. They'd be in visual range with the satellites in only fifteen seconds, and Paul had already turned his attention back on him. There was no time for anything else, nothing to do but execute John's order. He rapidly initiated the program, said a quick prayer, and pressed the Enter button on his keyboard.

Immediately, the ship began to shudder.

Paul had time to say "What the hell?"

Beth shouted "No, Dan!"

But Dan remembered what John had said. At all costs – keep the ship secret. Keep it safe. And Dan trusted John like no other.

A beam of light shot from the bow of the ship, stabbing the night ahead of them. In its passage, a kaleidoscope of colors blossomed into being, opening like a pinwheel of blazing light. Dan's eyes traced the swirling patterns as the ship shot into the middle of the maelstrom, rocketing down the cone shaped passage formed by the wormhole drive. A moment was all he had, though.

Because after that, they were...elsewhere.

FIFTEEN

The *Satori* made a keening noise, wailing like a banshee as she jumped out of the wormhole into real space. Dan felt like his mind had been turned inside out. He was dizzy, disoriented, and more than a little nauseated. Distantly, he could hear someone throwing up. He felt a heavy grip on the back of his chair. Paul's hand. Which meant Paul's gun had to be disturbingly close as well. Adrenaline soared through him, bringing clarity to his thoughts. The latches which held his wheelchair in place were designed to release quickly. If he could take Paul by surprise before the man could recover from the wormhole jump, he might have a chance.

He reached down with both hands, slapped the

release buttons, and then shoved back with every-thing he had.

He looked over one shoulder as he shoved, to see where Paul was standing: directly behind him, with a dazed look on his face. The wheelchair hit Paul hard in the thighs. Paul's hand – and the pistol! – were just in reach. Dan grabbed for the gun. He got hold with one hand, then with both. But as soon as Dan got a grip on the weapon, Paul seemed to wake up to what was going on, and Dan had to struggle to keep hold.

Paul wasn't a small man, and he used his weight, trying to wrest the gun away. Dan tried to smash Paul's elbow against his shoulder, but Paul twisted his arm so that it glanced off. Dan could feel his fingers slipping.

Then he snapped an elbow into Dan's temple, and again into the back of his head as he tried to turn away. Dan saw stars. He realized he'd lost his grip on the gun entirely, and opened his eyes, fighting to focus on his adversary.

Paul had backed up two steps, the gun held very professionally in a two handed grip, trained on Dan's head. His mouth twisted in a snarl.

"That was a mistake, Dan," Paul said.

Still dizzy from the blows, Dan replied "No kidding, shithead. Ow."

"You could have killed us all. What did you use for jump coordinates?" Paul asked.

"Didn't have time to input any. Blind jump, lowest power setting."

"You asshole," Paul said.

"Says the guy pointing a gun at me."

"It was my order. You want to be mad at someone, get mad at me," John said. He was struggling back to his feet, hands still zip-tied together.

"Boys and their toy guns. We need to figure out what our status is," said Charline. "Majel, where are we?"

"Proximate to Jupiter. Decaying orbit, entering upper atmosphere in three minutes," replied the computer.

That wasn't good. Relieved as he felt that they'd come through the wormhole intact, Jupiter could make them just as dead. Dan turned back to his console to get the ship back under control before they were cooked or crushed by the gas giant. He heard a metallic clicking sound, and froze before his hands could touch anything. He lifted hands from the controls slowly, and turned his head to face Paul. The gun was still trained at his head, and Paul had just pulled the hammer back.

"Don't even think about touching those controls," Paul said.

Dan tried to remain calm. Which was a difficult thing to manage while he was staring down the barrel of a pistol. He swallowed hard. "Paul... I need to stop our descent or we're toast."

Warning lights began flashing across his console, and the ship shuddered a little. They were breaching the upper atmosphere. Dan felt sure the engines had enough power to get them out of this, but it was going to be tight if he couldn't get started right away. If Jupiter yanked them deep enough into its gravity well, did the Satori's engines have enough strength to get them clear? He wasn't sure, and this wasn't a good time to test their engine strength.

"I'll do it. You can give me directions." Paul switched to a one handed grip on the gun, reached into a pocket and withdrew another zip-tie. "Put these on."

JOHN KNEW he had to intervene. He had faith Dan could pilot the ship safely away, but Paul? It was a miracle they'd survived the blind jump. He wasn't going to ask for a second one this soon. John took a step toward Paul, careful not to make any sudden moves. Even the small step got Paul's immediate attention.

"You can't really expect Dan to talk you through this, can you? Have you ever flown a ship out of a gas giant before?" John asked.

Another step, and then Paul pivoted the pistol toward him instead.

"Neither has he," Paul said.

"No one has. But Dan's about as good as they get, and he's our best shot. Tie him up, and we're all dead."

"You're not in charge here anymore, John." Paul locked eyes with John.

"The hell I'm not. Now cut Charline's cuffs so she can work with Majel to get us a course out of this mess."

Paul's face grew red. "You're still not taking me seriously? Now? I think I need to show everyone who's really in charge." His finger moved to the trigger. "Goodbye, John."

John froze. He couldn't make himself move. All he he could see was the round hole at the business end of the pistol as Paul steadied his hand and aimed the weapon directly at his head. He felt Beth tense behind him, preparing to strike. She wouldn't be able to throw the bullet off course, though. Even if the crew somehow overpowered Paul, it wasn't going to save him. John knew he was about to die. He could see the certainty of his death in Paul's eyes.

And then a hand sliced down into Paul's wrists, snapping the gun out of his fingers. It clattered heavily on the deck plates, but didn't go off. It was Andrew. John could see blood caking his hair where he'd been hit. Even injured, he was on his feet.

"I'm not very happy with you right now, Paul," Andrew said. His voice was flat and cold as the weapon Paul had been holding a moment before.

Paul growled and took a swing at him. Andrew ducked inside, blocked the blow with a forearm, and thrust the heel of his palm into Paul's face. Without missing a beat, Andrew grabbed the other man's shoulders and pulled him forward, right knee rising to smash into his gut as it descended. Paul groaned as all his air huffed out.

Then Andrew glided sideways, still holding Paul's body as it continued its forward movement. His right arm slipped past Paul's head, and he brought that elbow crashing into the back of Paul's skull. In a handful of seconds the fight was over. Paul fell to the deck, unmoving.

"Thanks, Andrew," John said. His voice had a little shake to it, but he was glad it wasn't too bad.

"That's why you pay me the big bucks, John," Andrew replied. "Sorry. Can't believe I let him get the drop on me." He produced a knife from somewhere and cut John's cuffs.

John wanted to tell Andrew that he was so much more than just an employee to him. But it wasn't the right time.

Somehow, it never seemed to be the right time for the things that were important.

SIXTEEN

As soon as Dan saw Paul was down, he dropped the zip-ties that he'd never put on and put his eyes back on his controls. The windows ahead showed nothing but stars. They were falling tail-first into Jupiter's atmosphere, and accelerating as they dropped.

"How bad is it?" John asked, rubbing his wrists. The ship was beginning to shake more.

"Ask me again in a minute or so," Dan replied.

Dan checked his scan readings, trying to get his bearings. The ship was starting to roll a little, nose turning as it was buffeted by high atmosphere winds. He quickly saw wisps of orange vapor streaming past. The ship shook hard as it was buffeted by one particularly strong blast of wind, and then before he knew it the ship was nose down toward Jupiter. The planet loomed, vast and over-whelming in the ship's front windows.

"That won't do," Dan muttered.

Dan pulled up hard on the flight controls. Stars came back into the front window, and he engaged the engines, slowly adding more power. The engines thrummed in response, pushing the ship away from the planet below. They were making good headway. He plotted a course which would put them into a safe orbit around the gas giant.

Dan heaved a sign of relief. One problem solved. Remembering the other problems, he turned and looked around at the rest of the crew.

Andy and John were wrestling Paul's limp form over to the wall next to Paul's seat. Charline was bent over her console working on something – someone had cut her hands free – and Beth... Well, Beth was glaring at him.

"That was a hell of a risk!" she said. "You sent us into a blind wormhole? We could have ended up anywhere!"

"It was John's orders. That's what he meant when he said 'ad astra'. But we weren't totally blind."

"Not totally," said Charline. She punched

some keys, calling up an image on her screen, then pressed another key to transmit the same image to Beth's console. "You knew Majel has managed to translate some of the database from the original ship's computer core. Working with Dan and Majel, I got coordinate locks for all these destinations." The screen displayed scores of different symbol strings, in a variety of different colors.

"Majel managed to extrapolate some data about jumps in general from that mess," Dan went on. "It's not much, but Charline and I wrote an emergency protocol in case we ever needed a fast and dirty jump to get out of Dodge quickly. The program powers up the smallest possible charge to the wormhole generator, so that we're popped straight forward a few AUs at most."

He blinked. "Well, more like six AUs this time. Looks like the short wormhole was impacted by Jupiter's gravity well, maybe." Who knew all those astrophysics classes from college would pay off?

"I did the coding, but I don't have Dan's background in astrophysics. Team effort," Charline added.

Beth studied the screen for another moment. "Seems like you two have spent a lot of time together on this," she said. "Planning to tell the engineer about it anytime soon?"

"It was all preliminary stuff, Beth," Dan said. "I never dreamed we'd use it on the first flight."

There was an uncomfortable pause. None of them had been expecting anything like this for their first trip out. The plan had been to take the ship out, do a shakedown cruise using the gravity engines only, and then return to go over the data. Testing the wormhole drive had never been on the agenda. Well, Paul's actions had accelerated their agenda a lot.

"So, the million dollar question is – can we jump back?" Charline asked.

"I wouldn't recommend it," Beth said. "I don't pretend to know precisely how the wormholes work, but Dan might be on to something about the gravity well reshaping the wormhole. If it's true that the less power we put into the wormhole, the more it is affected by gravity – and we aim a low power wormhole inward toward the sun – then the sun's gravity will pull the wormhole a lot more than Jupiter did..."

"...and we might end up a crispy critter," Dan finished for her. "Damn. I just realized – what if the nose of the ship had happened to be facing in-system instead of out when we jumped?"

"I don't even want to think about it," John said.

"Makes the most sense to just use the regular drive, then," Dan said. "It might make for a longer trip, but we'll be more sure to get where we're going."

"One problem," Charline said. Everyone looked over at her. "Isn't the cloaking device still broken? If we just fly the ship from Jupiter back to Luna - I can't believe I just said that sentence - won't someone see us?"

"Probably," Beth replied. "I'm going to bet that Paul did something to muck with the cloak. What-ever he did shouldn't be too difficult to fix. I'll get on that next."

"And when Paul wakes up I can have a little chat with him. I'll bet I can get him to consider telling you what he did, if you have problems," Andy said, cracking his knuckles.

"So, we fix whatever Paul did to the cloak, then we cruise back to Luna. We've certainly given the ship a bigger shakedown than we'd intended. And we can get a good feel for how fast *Satori* can go on her gravity drive," John said.

Dan saw Andy snatch the gun from the deck and stick it into a pocket, then grab a spare zip tie from the unconscious Paul and cuff him to a stanchion. He was starting to moan and come around again. Dan wondered what they should do with him now. What *could* they do with him, in the long run? He knew about the ship. Letting him go would mean exposing its existence to the world. They seemed to be in agreement that would be a bad plan. But locking him up with no trial, no timetable for release? That didn't seem just, either. Dan snapped the latches back into place, fastening his wheelchair to his console. He checked their present location and course, gently making a few adjustments. They could worry about what to do with Paul in the long term later. For now, getting the ship and crew home safely had to remain the top priority.

"Got us stabilized into a low orbit," Dan said. "Soon as Beth gets the cloak fixed and Majel finishes calculating the course for home, we can be on our way."

SEVENTEEN

Paul came to, groggy at first. What had happened to him? He'd been struck. Knocked out by that big lout John kept around as muscle. Paul had never liked Andy. The man reminded him too much of the bullies he'd faced when he was younger. Now there was even more reason than before to feel that way about him. He groaned a little and then stifled the sound quickly. Better that the rest of the crew still thought he was out.

He was cuffed to the wall. With one of his own damned zip-ties, to add insult to injury. It wasn't going to be quick or easy to get out of that. He listened to the murmur of conversation from his ship-mates. They were talking over how to get back home again. They figured it was over. They'd won, he was tied up and not going anywhere, and that was the end of the matter.

What were they going to do with him when they got back? He listened, but didn't hear anyone mention their thoughts or plans about his future. They weren't just going to hand him over to the authorities on Earth. They couldn't do that. He knew too much. They would never let him go. The very best he could hope for was that they would stick him in some cell at the bottom of Caraway's cursed base and leave him there to rot.

But even then he would be a security liability. No, the smart move would be to make him vanish. He'd be reported as lost, killed in some sort of accident. Maybe his body would be reported as 'sucked out into space' and unrecoverable. Or maybe his remains would be burned beyond recognition. Whatever the case was going to be, Paul was pretty sure he wasn't going to live through this screwup. They couldn't afford to keep him alive. John might talk the talk about his honor and doing the right thing. But at the end of the day he was just like everyone else. He'd look out for his own interests first.

How had things gone so badly? He had this

plan. It should have worked perfectly. He knocked out the biggest physical threat, and then had the gun to deal with the others. If they'd tried to play tough, he had the explosives to fall back on. Paul hadn't counted on Dan coming up with a crazy wormhole jump halfway across the solar system. That had been where things started to come unraveled. Anger surged, almost overwhelming him. He wanted to yank his hands, try to free himself, but Paul knew that wasn't going to get him anywhere. No, he needed to play this smart. He had to out-think the others.

Besides, he still had the explosives in play. He rolled a little, the small movement not attracting any attention, but it let him get his bound hands close to his chest pocket. That's where the trigger was. He fished the little thing free and palmed it. Time to take some action. Once the first bombs went off, they would know he was serious. If they wanted to avoid the others blowing up the entire ship, they would need to make a deal with him. Only he could disarm the rest of the explosives before they went off.

Paul risked a quick glance at the rest of the crew, just breaking up from their little conference. At first no one noticed him sitting there, watching them. Then Beth stood up from her console to head back toward her engines. She was so lost in thought that even she missed seeing he was awake. Paul laughed. He couldn't help himself. This was going to work. He'd regain control of the situation, get them all tied up, and then they would return to Earth. He'd have his hero's welcome after all. It was risky, but the alternative was either death or a lifetime locked in a private cell. Neither option was appealing. It was worth taking chances to avoid those fates.

Beth turned and looked at Paul. Andy had done a number on his face. He could feel it swelling, and it hurt like hell. He must appear awful, too, judging by the look on Beth's face. Whatever; he didn't need her approval anymore. She'd given him her last order. Paul leered at her from a shattered face with a hideous grin. Then her eyes widened. She'd seen what he was holding. Beth always was one of the brighter minds in this bunch. Too bad she was still too slow, and on the wrong side. He held the little pen-like device out where she could see it clearly.

"Did you really think all I had here was a gun?" Paul asked.

He lifted it upright in front of his face. Anyone

looking at the thing would think it was just a pen, and it would even write in a pinch. Paul loved the irony of hiding something crucial in plain sight. He'd done so with the explosives, disguising them as bolts. And he'd done it with his detonator as well. An old spy film had given him the idea, featuring a clicking pen that exploded if clicked just right.

"Stop him!" Beth shouted.

Andy was up and moving before she finished speaking. Beth dashed across the bridge as she yelled, trying to get to Paul, but neither of them were going to reach him in time. His thumb pressed down hard on the button. The world seemed to roll by in slow motion.

Sparks flew from the console in front of Dan, arcs of electricity jumping from the controls, tossing his body against the back of his chair. The entire board blew out, blasting bits of smoldering plastic all around the room.

Then a larger explosion rocked the ship. The deck seemed to buck beneath Paul, surging from the blast. He cracked his head against the wall beside him. Stars danced in front of his eyes. He felt his ears pop as he slumped to the floor. That meant there was a pressure loss somewhere in the rear of the ship. Hatches snapped shut automatically, and cut off the air loss. Just as he had known they would. The artificial gravity failed next. Paul felt his body floating free from the floor and wall. Beth had been knocked across the room by the blast. Although Andy kept his feet under him, he was now drifting in the middle of the room, reaching out to try to grab any hand-hold he could find.

The main drive was down, and they were out of control. He saw Jupiter appear in the front windows again, and then slip away. They were starting to spin, which wasn't helping his aching head. Their pilot was out of commission, the engines were offline, and the blast must have caused them to break from the stable orbit Dan had just said he'd put them in. Sweat broke out on Paul's forehead. He hadn't planned on getting them all killed with this stunt! He wanted to recover control so he could stay alive, not wind up crushed into paste by Jupiter.

"Surrender or we're all going to die," Paul said, holding the detonator up where they could all see it.

EIGHTEEN

Beth managed to grab hold of something to stop herself from bumping around. The ship was badly hurt. She could tell that without even checking. Something critical had been sabotaged by that blast. There were only so many places on the ship that one small explosive - she could tell that it was small because they were all still alive - would so completely knock out their systems. Repairing the problem might be difficult, but it shouldn't be impossible. But Paul was brandishing that detonator like it was a weapon. That meant he had to have other bombs he could set off.

They had to stop him before he could blow the ship.

"Detonator in his hand!" Beth called out.

John was still strapped into his seat. He released his straps and held on to his chair with one hand while he grabbed Andy's foot with the other, hauling him back toward the deck.

"Andrew!" John said. "Sedate that bastard. And then strap him up well enough that he can't pull anything else. Make sure he's got no more tricks handy, while you're at it. I don't care if you have to strip him."

"Consider it done," Andy said, advancing on Paul with a menacing look.

"No!" Paul shouted. "Wait!"

"I've had enough of this," Andy said. He yanked the pen device out of Paul's hand and snapped it in half. Then he tore a strip of duct tape from a roll and slapped it across Paul's mouth.

Beth let go of the rail she'd been holding and pushed off toward Dan's chair. She grabbed hold of it and checked his neck for a pulse. It was there, still beating solidly. Her shoulders relaxed, and she exhaled with relief. He had small burns on his face and bits of hot plastic had singed the front of his jumpsuit, but he was alive. She couldn't very well detach his wheelchair from the console and let him drift around, so she worked around him, checking the extent of the damage to the flight controls. The answer didn't take long. The controls were trashed. She'd need to rebuild them from scratch, or close to it. They could re-route control to another console, but this one was toast. Whatever Paul had used as an explosive was both small and effective.

"Got the med kit," Charline said, pushing off from the wall. She glided over to Beth, who helped her stop. Charline pulled a small medical scanner out of the kit and placed it on Dan's chest. Then she rummaged around in the kit for a moment.

"Andy, catch," she said, and gently sent a capped syringe floating toward him. "Use it on that jerk."

Paul continued thrashing ever more wildly. Andy injected the syringe into Paul's arm, and he went limp again. He pulled out some more duct tape and set about making sure Paul wouldn't cause any more trouble.

Beth turned back to Charline, who was expertly pulling out packets from the kit. She applied a salve to Dan's burns, and steri-strips to a few of the larger cuts on his face. Charline peeked at the monitor beeping away on Dan's chest periodically like she knew what the thing's readout was telling her. Beth nodded in approval.

"You've done this sort of thing before?" Beth asked.

"I worked as an EMS volunteer in college," Charline replied with a shrug. "I'm no doctor, but doing this sort of field medicine is like riding a bicycle. He's going to be OK."

"A woman of hidden talents. I'm impressed," Beth said. Inwardly she felt an enormous relief at hearing Dan would be all right. When Charline frowned, Beth went on to reassure her. "I mean that. I'm glad you're here."

Charline smiled back with a warmth that lit up her face. "Thanks. You'll forgive me if I sort of wish I wasn't, though. This sort of adventure wasn't really what I signed up for!"

"None of us did," Beth chuckled. The woman's humor had broken at least a little of the tension she'd been feeling.

John was flipping switches on his console, tapping his keyboard, trying to bring something up, but Beth could see there wasn't enough electricity reaching the bridge. The only power left in the room was emergency lighting, which was powered by local batteries. Even the vents which cycled fresh air through the ship had stopped hissing. Life support was out. Which was going to make the air a little stale soon, if they didn't slide back into Jupiter's embrace first.

"How bad is it?" asked John.

"Dan's OK. The console is shot," Beth replied.

"Well, at least Dan's OK. What do you think that second explosion was, Beth?" John asked.

She thought a moment. "Most likely, it was a charge set near the coupling between the alien and human technologies. That's always been our weak spot. It's a choke point, the most devastating point of failure for the ship. I'd meant to put in a backup, but never had time. So everything went through one cable."

"One point of failure also means one place to fix. Might make the repair easier?" Andy asked.

"If that's where it blew. Probably was. He is – was – one of our lead engineers. He knew exactly where to hit us to disable the ship," Beth said. How could she have not seen this coming? She wasn't the sort to trust just anyone. How had Paul managed to slip under her paranoia radar? "I'll get suited up and go check. I can use the central corridor as an airlock."

"Sounds good, but be careful. We can't afford to

lose you," said John. "At the same time, alacrity would be excellent. Without the ship's sensors we have no idea how bad this really is – but we're too close to Jupiter for comfort. We have to assume that even if we're not actively falling yet, our orbit is going to decay fast. Time is short."

Beth rolled her eyes. "So you want me to be cautious but quick?"

"In a nutshell, yes," John replied. He showed the first smile she had seen from him since Paul drew his pistol.

"Charline, try to see if you can route a little of the backup power to a computer terminal," John said, "Get us something. Even a little power might help. Andy, keep an eye on the prisoner and Dan. Beth, I'll come back there with you. I might not be an engineer, but I can hand you tools and maybe help if there's any heavy lifting. I can keep touch with everyone as easily by radio from there as anyplace else. Let's go, folks."

Beth glanced out the front windows and saw Jupiter glide past again, and then slowly vanish. They were still in a spin. Out of control and turning wildly in space, they almost had to be either getting closer to the gas giant or drifting away from it. If it was the latter, they had plenty of time to figure this mess out. Beth wasn't counting on that, though. She was pretty sure Jupiter was growing larger in that view every time they rolled over so that she could see it. John was right. They were running out of time.

NINETEEN

C harline hooked a leg over the arm of her chair, then reached over to pull away the panel covering her console. She'd been weightless before, but she still wasn't used to this floating around thing. On the moon, she'd still had an up and a down, at least. Sliding under the console, she bounced off the floor a bit and had to steady herself. Her stomach was roiling. This whole zero gravity thing was going to take more getting used to before she was really going to be OK with it.

How the hell had she ended up in this mess, anyway? A month ago she had a nice, cushy job on Earth with a major tech corporation. One asshole made a move on her, and she ended up fired, in space, and lost in a damaged starship someone badly wanted to either destroy or capture. Paul didn't really seem particular which result he got, either. This wasn't what she had signed on for. Cloak and dagger stuff was awesome in the movies, but in real life it just sucked.

Charline remembered reading somewhere that the definition of an adventure was uncomfortable things happening to strangers far away. They felt a whole lot less like an adventure and a lot more uncomfortable when it was your life on the line instead of a character in a movie. Just then she'd have given nearly anything to have her feet back on solid ground again. But if she wanted to get back home, she was going to need to find a way to help them solve the stack of problems they faced. She reached out for some wires, and the movement sent her head bouncing against the floor again.

"FML," Charline muttered under her breath.

"You OK in there?" Andy asked.

"Not really, no. I'm a hacker, not an electrician," Charline said. "You want someone who knows the ins and outs of computer security? I'm your girl. But John wants me to hook up one of these terminals to a backup battery. Actually, to several batteries, since one of them isn't going to give me enough juice to power it."

"Can you do it?" Andy asked.

"Yeah, I think so," Charline replied as she popped out from beneath the console. She pushed off and floated over to the ruins of Dan's computer and flight controls. She was going to need wire. Lots and lots of wire. Hotwiring this thing to work off battery power would be a pain in the ass, and the best she could hope for was a cobbled together system that might run for a short while. But it would give them something, at least.

Charline grabbed a tool and used it to cut several arm-lengths of electrical wire out of the broken console. The wire was scorched by the explosion, and the rubber coating was torn in some places. She'd need to test each strand to make sure it was still conducting electricity properly before she could use it to patch the batteries together and wire them into the terminal. Even if she could get this console working again, they still wouldn't have control of the ship. She wasn't sure this was going to do any good. But it was better than sitting there doing nothing.

She glanced over at Dan, checking the monitor on his chest. At least he was going to be OK. The medical scanner said his heart rhythm was fine, and that was her biggest worry after the shock he'd taken. When the console blew it had shorted out, sending a charge through him since he'd been touching the thing. Charline had cleaned him up pretty well. He ought to wake up on his own before too long, and his wounds were all clean and patched up. She hadn't used those skills in a while, and patching him up felt good.

Once she'd pulled what she guessed would be enough wiring to do the job out of the trashed console, Charline pulled out her tablet and had it display schematics for the ship. Hunting around for the backup batteries would take too long, and unlike Beth she hadn't designed the Satori, so she didn't know where all the parts were by heart. Another reason why she was probably the wrong person for this job… But it wasn't like she could do what Beth was trying to accomplish, either. Charline figured she'd have to muddle along as best she could and hopefully get this to work without frying herself in the process. The batteries should be stored behind a closed maintenance panel set into the ceiling in the center of the control room. Which would have been a pain to access, if they still had gravity. But without it?

Charline pushed off from Dan's console and floated over to the panel the schematics indicated. When she got there, she stared at the big plate in frustration.

"Something wrong?" Andy asked.

"Who the hell uses hex bolts to put something together?" Charline asked.

"Beth, apparently?"

"Well, I have Philip's head and standard screwdrivers on my multitool. I don't have a hex key," Charline said. She was getting exasperated with the whole trip. The string of problems they'd run into were enough to melt your mind. It wasn't enough to have a member of the team turn on them with a gun, no. He had to have planted explosives on the ship and managed to set them off. But only after they'd gone halfway across the solar system, so far from help that they might as well be in another galaxy.

"Here, got you covered," Andy said, tossing a small case up to her. The plastic box glided through the air. Charline caught it with her free hand.

"What is it?" she asked.

"Hex key set, among other things. Basic repair kit. Every room on the ship has one of those, a first aid kit, a fire extinguisher, and oxygen masks.

Emergency gear, for, well, times like these," Andy replied.

The back of the box was covered with velcro which let Charline attach it to a pad on her thigh. She opened it up and carefully pulled out the tool she needed to remove the panel. Charline kept her hands moving slowly despite the urgent need to hurry this job up. They needed at least one computer on the ship powered up again very badly, but if she fumbled a tool and it went sailing off across the room in microgravity, it wasn't going to get the job done faster. She took a deep breath and tried vainly to relax.

"Slow is smooth, smooth is fast," she said in a soft voice.

"Heh," Andy chuckled, apparently overhearing her.

"What's so funny?"

"We used to say that back in the Army. But there, we were usually talking about clearing a room or bunker, not electronics work!" he replied.

Charline smiled down at him. Andy had strapped himself into one of the chairs to avoid floating around. He'd stuck close to Paul, for which she was grateful. Having him around when that jerk woke up would be a real plus. There was something about Andy's manner that just made her want to trust him.

"You ever wish you'd never come out here at all?" she blurted.

"Not really, no. I owe John too much. If I can help keep him alive through this mess, I'll consider it worth doing," Andy said.

"You really think we can get out of this?" Charline asked.

"We've got one of the best engineers in the world, one of the best pilots in the world, one of the best computer people in the world, and the most advanced spaceship humanity has ever created. I think we've got a better than even chance," Andy replied.

His words made her feel a little better. Charline still wasn't sure just how they were going to make it all work out, but trying was better than giving up. While they were still breathing, there was a chance. She'd fight every step of the way to keep that chance alive.

"Got a couple of batteries hooked together," she said. "Now to test them."

Charline connected two wires together, hoping to see a spark from the contact. Nothing. This was going to take a lot of work.

TWENTY

The suit felt clunky around her. Beth realized that she'd been spending too much time in Lunar gravity. And too much time in an air-filled hangar. Oh, she'd logged enough hours in zero gee, and enough in a suit. But that was before the project. So now, when it counted, everything felt a little rusty. Assuming they ever got out of this Beth made herself a promise that she'd spend more time working in a suit. She was about to have to do a whole bunch of emergency repair work wearing the thing, and fumble-fingers wasn't going to make this project any easier.

She checked the seals on John's suit. He was even slower getting suited up than she was, but not by a lot. He'd obviously made an effort to train with the equipment. How he'd found time for it, she had no idea. His suit checked out perfectly, though, as did her own when he went over it for problems. Both suits good, she checked the seals for all the doors off the main corridor. The central passage led just about everywhere in the ship, with storage, bunk rooms, an arms locker, galley, closet sized infirmary, and other spaces leading from it.

On one end of the long corridor was the bridge. On the other, the engine room. It wasn't a large ship, and they wouldn't lose a ton of air when they dumped it from the hallway, provided they could prevent leaks from the rest of the ship. The central hallway would act like an airlock from the rest of the ship to the airless engine room.

Once she was sure every hatch was sealed, she tried to open the engine room door. It had sealed shut automatically when it sensed the pressure loss, and the hard seal required a computer override. The problem was, the computers were down, so the little access panel on the side of the door was dead.

Not a huge issue for Beth. She always kept a few tools handy. She pulled a screwdriver from its place in a loop on her thigh, adjusted the head, and a few moments later had pulled the face from the panel. Inside was a hash of little circuit boards and wires. The tangled mess was a maze, but she'd helped install the things. She knew how they worked.

A couple of moments and a short circuit later, the hatch popped open a few inches. Air rushed from the corridor, sucking John against a wall, but neither of them were in any danger in their suits. Once the air had evacuated, she pulled herself up to the gap and pushed with both hands. The doors didn't slide easily, but they went back far enough that they were both able to get inside the engine area.

She inhaled with a low whistle when she got a good look at her engine room.

"I was right about where he hit us. Wish I wasn't," Beth said over the suit radio. Those had internal power, so she and John could still speak to each other. It looked like the damage was focused precisely where she'd thought it would be. How Paul managed to get a bomb in here, she wasn't sure. But the damage had been precisely calculated to hit them right where it hurt the most. The explosion had ripped the floor to bits about midway down the conduit connecting the human and alien tech. There was no backup for that line. Installing a second conduit was something Beth had been planning to do, but John's accelerated schedule made her set the idea aside in favor of higher priority tasks.

Part of her wanted to round on him with a hearty 'I told you so', but that wasn't going to help anyone. The damage was done, and it was up to her to undo it. There would be plenty of time for her to give him shit over this later, assuming they all survived this mess.

"Stay here a minute while I survey the damage," Beth told John. Starting with the cloak, since that's what had failed first. She needed to assess the damage one step at a time – slow is smooth, smooth is fast. She pulled the metal cover from the cloaking device. Paul had tampered with it, all right. It was a quick bit of sabotage. Obviously he'd set this up so that the cloak could be quickly reactivated, and the ship safely vanished to wherever it was he'd intended to bring it.

The alien tech was...odd was too light a word. Rather than using printed circuit boards and microscopic transistors, like human tech did, they used small cubes, about the size of the dice for a board game. The theory was that each was some sort of quantum computing device. But they had to be sequenced in the right order. Putting them together in the first place had been like assembling a puzzle with a hundred pieces, each identical to all the others. It had taken months, because they'd been jumbled all over the interior of the device.

To prevent future problems of the same sort, she'd used a marker on each one. Simple. But effective. She tested with washable ink at first, but when the device still worked without any problems, she switched to a permanent marker.

And that made spotting the sabotage simple. The cubes for sixty six and ninety nine had been swapped, both installed upside down so that they looked about right. But she knew her own handwriting. She swapped both cubes back, and that was one problem out of the way. She carefully replaced the cover.

"Cloak is back online. It was a quick fix. I can activate it from here, in a pinch, but I don't think that's a major problem right now," she said.

"No, this is," John said, waving at the mess the bomb had made of the main conduit.

"Hey, how's it going back there?" Andy's voice cut in over their radios. "I grabbed another suit so I could keep a radio link with you two."

"The cloak was an easy fix. The rest of it's not

going to be so simple. We're getting to it now. I'll see what I can patch fast, and what's going to take more time," she replied.

"OK," Andy said. "Let me know if there's anything I can do. Looks like Dan is starting to come around, going to go check on him now."

Beth couldn't help feeling a sense of relief about Dan. She'd been more worried about him than she was willing to let on, even to herself. She shoved her roiling emotions about her ex aside. There was a job to do here, and she needed her head in the game. Beth knelt by the damaged conduit and went to work. The air in the bridge was going to get thin really fast if she couldn't get life support operating again soon. Not to mention the gas giant they were coasting along next to, just waiting to suck them down and crush them into a little ball. No pressure, she told herself. Just the lives of every person on the ship at stake.

TWENTY-ONE

A ndy breathed a sigh of relief as Dan's eyelids began to flutter. He knew that Charline had been peeking at the medical monitor periodically. She'd told him more than once that Dan was just unconscious, and that it was best to let him sleep it off. He'd come around when his body was ready to wake up. That hadn't made it any easier to sit around passing her tools and watching two sleeping men. He felt more than a little useless. Everyone else on the ship was helping get them out of this mess, and him? Andy was supposed to be the security specialist. It was his job to stop things like Paul's scheme from happening in the first place, and he'd failed utterly in that duty. He watched Dan's eyelids move again and heard the pilot give soft moan.

"It's about time you woke up," Andy said. Dan coughed twice, his whole body shaking in the action, then slowly opened his eyes.

"What hit me?" Dan asked.

"Your console did. Blew up in your face," Charline said. "How are you feeling?"

"Ow," Dan said.

"Ow is right," Andy said, chuckling. "I'd give you some water, but we're in zero gee right now, and the zero-gee water bulbs are on the other side of an airless corridor."

"S'OK. I'll be all right in a minute," Dan said, closing his eyes again. Then they snapped open. "My console blew? How'd that happen?"

Andy gave Paul a hard look where the man was still floating, zip tied to the wall. Paul was awake again too, although he seemed bleary and lethargic from the sedative. "Ask Paul. Looks like he had more than a gun."

Dan was staring around at the bridge, which only dimly illuminated by emergency lights. He looked a little lost. Andy couldn't blame him. When he'd been knocked out they had everything under control again. Then those explosions…

"I'll bring you up to speed," Andy said. "Your console blew, and another bomb in the engine room went off. Beth and John are back there trying to repair the main conduit. Charline is over there hoping to get a little power from the emergency systems, give us something."

Charline looked up from her work with a relieved smile and waved. "Welcome back."

"We're in a spin, it looks like our orbit is degrading, and we have no power, so there's no way to access the alien systems," he finished.

"Like the engines we need to get us out of this mess," Dan said.

"Exactly," Andy said.

Paul was making more noise over there on the wall. Andy eyed him suspiciously. He was rocking back and forth, and it looked like he was growing increasingly agitated despite the drugs. His mouth was opening and closing under the tape Andy had slapped over it, and he was frantically bopping about, but the lack of gravity was making his movements into a confused jumble.

"What's his problem?" asked Dan.

"Not sure," Andy said. He pushed off from Dan's chair, gliding effortlessly to the wall near Paul. Paul's eyes were bulging now, and he was gesturing wildly at his gag with both bound hands. He was still breathing OK, so that wasn't the problem. Andy's eyes narrowed. He moved closer cautiously, looking for but not seeing any trap.

"It looks like he wants to say something, Andy," Dan said, eying Paul from his seat.

That was exactly what it looked like. Andy shrugged a little. Couldn't hurt to let him have his say. Probably. He leaned in toward Paul. "I'm going to take off the gag, Paul. If you piss me off, I'm going to put it back on, and add an extra couple yards of tape, wrapped around your head a few times. You get me?"

Paul's head bobbed up and down. Andy grabbed a corner of the tape and yanked hard.

"Ow!" Paul said.

"Less crying. What did you want to say so badly?" Andy asked.

Paul was breathing hard and fast, like he'd been running. He was beyond agitated. This was a panic reaction, Andy realized. He stayed alert for any sudden movements. People got unpredictable when they panicked, and Paul had been more than enough trouble already. He wasn't going to give the guy any more chances to create more problems for them.

"You have to understand," Paul said. "I wanted the ship. I wasn't going to hurt any of you if I could avoid it."

"Tell that to my skull," Andy said, rubbing the still-sore spot where Paul had knocked him out with one hand.

"Sorry for that. I really am. But our country needs this ship, don't you see? With the energy from this ship powering our electric grid, we could solve so many problems!" Paul said.

"By turning us over to your Marine friends?" Dan asked.

"There weren't really any marines – the security John put over communications was too tough. I was only able to clue the feds in that something worth watching was going down. That's why they repositioned the satellite."

"Best news I've heard all day," Andy said.

"But you don't understand!" Paul said. "There were four bombs!"

"What?"

Charline shouted in triumph. "Got it!"

The emergency lights flickered and dimmed, but her console came alive with power. Then she froze. She looked over at Paul and paled.

"What do you mean, four bombs? Where are the other two?" Andy asked.

"They're on the outside of the hull, down near the engines. My last ditch, to get you all to give it up. They're on timers. They ought to be going off soon. First one, then the other, about five minutes apart," Paul said. "They look like bolts. They've been inserted into the hull like any other bolt, to make them hard to spot."

"How do we disarm them?" Andy asked. He shook Paul's shoulders.

"You can't. You broke my remote," Paul said with a scowl.

The pen. Andy cursed under his breath. He'd broken it out of anger, and to keep Paul from using it to pull any more tricks. How much trouble had his temper landed them in? Damn it, this just kept getting worse. He felt his anger surge again and struggled to rein it in. Smacking Paul around might feel good, but it wasn't going to fix their problems. He needed to keep his cool to handle this situation.

"We ought to just space you, Paul, for all of this. You're lucky I don't have time right now," Andy replied.

"Charline, can you get any sort of read on our vector? How much trouble are we in?" Dan asked.

Leave it to the pilot to remember what was important right now, Andy thought. He was doubly glad Dan was awake and alert again. They needed his brains.

"Lots," she replied, still typing at high speed.

"How bad?" Dan said.

"Very. According to the computer, if we can't regain control soon, we'll be in the atmosphere. Maybe fifteen minutes. Once we hit that, the computer predicts we'll pick up downward speed rapidly as we lose our angular momentum."

Andy grabbed the suit helmet he'd used to talk to John and Beth. They weren't going to enjoy hearing this information any more than he had, but he needed to fill them in on what was going on. Plus he had an idea how these bombs were going to need to be dealt with. He didn't like it, but someone was going to have to go out there and pull the things off the ship, and that someone pretty much had to be him. Beth could maybe do it, but she was needed to repair the conduit. Andy had at least some experience with explosives from back when he was in the Army. It wasn't much, but it was probably more than Charline or Dan could boast of. There was no way Andy was letting John go out there to clean up the mess he'd allowed to happen.

"Hey, Beth? Charline got some power up, and she's tracking our descent. Our orbit is degrading fast. Fifteen minutes to atmosphere, and then things get nasty fast," Andy said. "On the plus side, Dan's awake again, so if you can get the engines running before we get cooked, he can fly us out of here."

"Great," came Beth's voice over the radio. "Nothing like pressure."

"That's not all though. Paul says he had two more bombs. On timers. Under your feet, from the sounds of it. I'm going to suit up and go outside to try to disarm them," Andy said.

John's voice came back "You sure that's the only way? He can't just turn them off?"

Andy looked at Paul. "He says no. Damned fool. Who sets bombs on a spaceship he'll be flying in? No, it looks like EVA or nothing."

"OK, Andrew. Get it done, but be careful," John said. "You'll all need to suit up – the corridor is depressurized, and I don't know if we can get the engine room door shut so you can pressurize it again. You're going to have to pump the air out of the bridge, too."

"Not a bad idea anyway," Dan said. He had already released himself from his wheelchair and was gliding over to the suit rack. "Spacesuits might save lives if another of those bombs goes off."

"Beth wants to get Majel back online," John said. "Charline, you can help her with that better than I can. I'll come forward to assist Andrew. Dan, you stay on the bridge. As soon as those drives come back on line, we need to get out of here."

Andy looked around the room, the thin haze of smoke still drifting in the missing gravity. He closed his eyes, trying to recall everything he'd ever learned about demolitions disposal. It had been a long, long time. He hoped it hadn't been too long.

He opened his eyes again. "OK, let's do this."

TWENTY-TWO

I t didn't take much time to get suited up. Funny how fast you can do something when there's so much on the line, Andy thought. He was glad he'd drilled so much in spacesuit use. It struck him as something that would probably be used infrequently, but when it was, he'd need to be quick. Dan was an old hand at EVA, and got into his suit faster than either he or Charline. He checked them both over, making sure the suits were perfect. Andy was pleased to get a sharp nod of approval from the man. He'd raced through the process of getting the suit on, and managed it without any errors.

Then came the more dangerous part. They

needed to at least try to get Paul into a suit. None of them were happy with him, but they didn't want him asphyxiating in front of their eyes, either. Dan held the gun on Paul while Andy stood by in case physical persuasion was required, but Paul put the suit on without complaint. The hardest part had been getting him zip tied back to the stanchion and taped up well enough that he couldn't give Dan any grief while Andy was 'outside'.

John came up the corridor and gave Charline a wave as she went by on her way to the engine room.

When she passed through the doorway to the engine room, John opened a private channel with Andy. "How are you feeling about this?"

"About the whole thing?" Andy laughed. "Not how I'd pictured this trip going, let's put it that way."

"My fault," John replied. "I should have seen trouble coming with Paul."

"He wasn't for keeping the ship, but I don't think anyone could have expected this out of him."

John shook himself a little. "Anyway, I was talking about the bomb disposal. Can you do this?" They stepped into the airlock and shut the inner door behind them. Andy started the airlock cycling. Most of the air had already evacuated from the ship through the holes in the engine room, so it didn't take long before the green light indicated they were clear to open the outer door.

"I think I can. Not like I have to disarm them; from what I got out of Paul, it sounds like I just need to pry them off the ship. Stay inside the airlock, though. Just in case," Andy said.

John reached out and placed a hand on each of Andy's shoulders. "Be careful."

"Better believe it."

Andy popped the outside hatch with the manual release – this airlock had been designed as an escape hatch, so it was hooked into the emergency power supply and had backup manual controls. A little residual air puffed out into space ahead of him.

Andy clipped one end of a safety line onto a steel ring just outside the airlock door. The other end was already attached to his suit. He slipped out of the airlock and flicked on his helmet lights. Parts of the ship were picking up light, either from the sun or reflected off Jupiter, but the ship was still slowly spinning, and that was putting different parts in and out of shadow. He played out some line and grasped a rail on the ship's hull, pulling himself hand over hand toward the engines. The suit had a small thruster pack, but he'd save that in case he really needed it.

The ship continued its slow spin, and Jupiter rolled beneath him. He froze, watching the planet slide into sight. The view was incredible, and took his breath away. He wasn't close enough to see individual clouds – and a voice in the back of his head was grateful for that! But he could see the whirling patterns moving through the clouds, swept around by winds stronger than any hurricane on Earth. Bands of color, patterns of light and shadow, twisting together with a savage beauty.

No one had ever seen Jupiter quite this way before. Video utterly failed to convey the enormity, the majesty, of this view.

"Beautiful, isn't it," John said. His tone made the question a statement.

"Yes," Andy said, embarrassed to be caught skylarking. Then the roll was moving the planet back out of view again, and he shook himself to get his head back in the game. Time was short, and everyone was counting on him.

The airlock was nearer to the nose than the aft of the ship, so it took him about a minute to reach the engine block. "I'm here. Going to start looking for the bombs now."

"Be careful, Andrew," John said.

The ship completed a spin, suspending him with Jupiter below his feet again, and he realized he didn't feel quite weightless anymore. There was a distinct pull from the huge planet below, a drag on his arms, until the spin went around again and he felt himself gently pushed back toward the hull instead. That was going to be a problem.

Now that he was feeling gravity, he'd have to work fast. Jupiter's pull would start dragging the ship down more rapidly, and make prying the bombs off more difficult for him as well. He went hand over hand across the hull, looking for a bolt that seemed out of place. Paul had told him how he'd disguised the small explosives. The bolts were shaped charges, so they'd blow mostly toward the point of the bolt, away from the head. Which meant these last two would direct their charges into the engine room itself. Beth and Charline were in there working. If the bombs blew, they could be killed. Worse yet, if the bombs blew the engine apart, or even damaged it enough, they were never going to get it working in time to escape Jupiter's pull.

There it was! He spotted the first one, and started pulling himself toward it. As he was moving, he saw the second as well. Both were a little off color from the other bolts. And where the others were all in neat, orderly rows, these two stood out, off on their own in the middle of plates. He stared at both bolts, trying to guess which one would blow first. Paul hadn't said. But one was closer to the alien engines than the other, so he guessed that one would blow last. Paul would have wanted to save the tech, if he could.

He settled himself near the device he thought would blow first, and hooked a snap carabiner around his safety line and a loop of metal bolted to the hull. At least someone had considered that deep space external repairs might be necessary. Just in time, too, as the ship swung around again, and he felt weight pulling him away from the ship. The line stopped him and held him in place, so he had both hands free to work.

He reached down to the velcro patch on his suit leg and pulled out a pair of tools. Charline had loaned him these back on the bridge – non conductive tools she used for dealing with the guts of computers. They might help prevent a static spark from jumping around as he worked. Sparks and explosives. Bad combination.

He worked one of the tools in between the bolt head and the hull, gently nudging the bolt free from the metal. It slid a tiny bit. Small motions, keep it small! There was a tiny gap now between the hull and the bolt head. Andy was sweating in his suit, acutely aware that the timer on the bolt might run out any second.

He was reaching down for another tool when his time ran out.

The bolt exploded, discharging most of its force into the hull, toward the engine room.

But enough force remained to blast the bolt head apart. There wasn't much of a shock wave, because there wasn't atmosphere around the ship to carry it, but the impact was still enough at point blank range to kick him back off the ship. That saved his life, as bits of hot metal whizzed by his suit instead of shredding the soft material.

For a terrible moment he felt like he was falling toward that huge planet below, unsure if anything would stop him. Then the line snapped taut, jerking him to a sudden stop. Andy's head cracked against the back of his helmet, sending new pain through his already sore skull. Stars danced in front of his vision, and he could taste blood in his mouth. The line held, but he dangled from the underside of the ship as it began to pick up speed, descending into the upper atmosphere of the enormous planet below.

TWENTY-THREE

One moment, Charline was squatting next to Beth, pulling a panel off a computer. The next, she found herself sprawled against one of the walls of the engine room as sections of torn deck smashed around her. Dizzy, she shook her head, trying to clear it, but the movement only made things worse. Her ears were ringing, and the coppery taste in her mouth told her she'd bitten something when she slammed into the wall. Charline panted, panic taking over for a few seconds. What had happened? Where was Beth?

"Beth? Can you hear me?" Charline said. There was no immediate response, but then John's voice came over her radio.

"You all right in there?" John said. "One of the other bombs went off."

The other bombs. Of course. That helped Charline calm her frayed nerves and take stock of her situation. She looked down at her suit's status readout on her wrist. Miraculously, the suit had no breaches; the thing was still intact. Charline thanked whatever god was out there keeping an eye on her for that. A hole in her suit would have been fatal. She glanced about at her surroundings. The engine room hadn't fared as well.

A section of the decking had torn upward, shards of hot metal pinging against the walls and ceiling. One larger chunk had blasted past her head to crash against the door Beth had hotwired to get in. It must have narrowly missed her faceplate. Door motors came briefly to life, as emergency systems within the door read the impact as a threat and strained to close the door again. The door shut with a grinding of metal on metal that she could feel in her boots.

Beth! She'd been right in front of the explosion. Was she all right? Charline looked for her in the dim light, the haze from the explosion making her search difficult. She spotted Beth floating near another wall, and pushed off toward her to help.

"You OK?" Charline asked.

"Yeah, I think so." Beth was checking the suit readout on her left wrist. "Shit."

"What? Are you hit?" Charline eyed her suit carefully, looking for a hole to patch.

"The suit says no punctures, but I think I lost a seal somewhere. I can hear a hissing noise."

"I can't patch that in here. We need to get you up to the bridge and get you into a new suit."

"No time," Beth said, turning back to her work. "We're almost out as it is. Can't you feel gravity starting to tug at us? We'll be flopping around in here with every spin of the ship before too long."

She ran wires from the power lines in the conduit over to the human mainframe. "I need Majel online fast. I think I have an idea. Can you get her rebooted, as soon as I get power to her system?"

Charline grinned weakly. She could reboot a computer in her sleep. "That, I can do."

Charline pulled herself over to a console that was hardwired to the mainframe and checked it out. It had been far enough from the explosion to be spared damage. In fact, she realized that most of the equipment in the room was undamaged. Paul's placement had been damned precise, or they'd just gotten really lucky. She had the feeling that last bomb would be another story, though. It sounded like that one was right underneath the alien tech. If it blew, Charline had no idea how much harm it would do to the alien power source, their drive, and all the other stuff housed back there. Hell, if it blew up the power unit the secondary explosion might kill them all. She shoved the thoughts away. It wasn't helping her focus. A flash of light told her Beth had restored power to the mainframe and her console. Charline typed out a series of rapid-fire commands, and the main computer began its reboot.

"OK, starting Majel's boot process. What now?" Charline asked.

Beth was back at work again. She grunted, pulling more wires apart with a shower of tiny sparks showing how hot they were. "I'm hoping to use Majel as a control interface. The wires to connect the bridge controls are a shambles, and it's going to take me hours to connect them all. But if I can hook up basic controls to Majel, we might be able to direct her using wifi from the bridge, and have her control the alien tech directly."

"So you want me to get our AI to interface directly with an alien computer that your best guys haven't been able to figure out with months to work on it. And I've got what, ten minutes?" Charline asked.

"More like five. But yeah. If you're up for it." Beth grinned. "If you can't, I don't know how we're getting out of this, short of going outside to push."

She noticed that Beth was panting a little. "How bad is that air leak?"

"Not as bad as it's going to be for all of us in a few minutes if I can't get those engines online. They were hit by some of the bits from the blast," Beth replied. "You worry about your impossible task, and let me worry about mine."

Charline raised an eyebrow, but turned back to the console, opening a command line interface and sending the signals to bring Majel back to life. That was the easy part. Once she had the program working again, she was going to need to figure out how to build an interface between human software and an alien computer that none of them understood in the slightest. In the space of a couple of minutes. This task wasn't just impossible, it was insane. Majel finished booting, and Charline started typing commands as fast as she could, making up the code as she went along.

Programming wasn't just about algorithms, it

was about language. At Charline's level of skill, code was art as well as science. If she could make this work it would be a masterpiece of effort. Totally focused on the task, she drove her fingers to fly over the keys.

TWENTY-FOUR

John had been completely shielded when the bomb went off. He hadn't even realized what had happened at first, but when he saw Andrew slammed backward, he knew something was terribly wrong. Just like everything else on this little jaunt – one wrong thing after another. Try as he might, he couldn't seem to get things back under control.

The safety line snapped taut, with Andrew dangling a couple of feet below the ship. Because he'd clipped in near where he was working, John couldn't just reel him back to the airlock. He was going to have to go out after Andrew himself. John clipped his own safety line to the airlock frame and started out toward his young friend. He growled, pulling himself along faster as the tug of gravity continued to increase. He had to get Andrew awake or back inside the *Satori*. The fact that they were feeling gravity at all meant that the ship's surface area was slowing their descent a little. If the ship was still falling toward the surface at the same speed as a rock, they'd still be weightless. But those broad wings were meeting some resistance already.

Which meant they were already reacting to Jupiter's upper atmosphere.

That didn't leave a lot of time before the ship started heating up. It wouldn't take long for things to go from 'heating up' to 'burning up'. They were almost out of time.

"Damn it, Andrew, wake up!" he said over the radio.

"Guh?"

"You're awake," John said, relief flooding his voice. "Are you hurt?"

"Uhhhh...yes?" Andy said. "But not too bad, I think. Going to be sore tomorrow though. My poor head!"

"Can you still stop the other bomb? We don't have much time."

"I'll give it a shot," he replied.

John reached out a hand to help him grab hold of the ship.

DAN WAS STARING AHEAD at the front windows. Jupiter rolled by, then back away again, then back into view. It was beginning to make him feel a little dizzy, but it was either that or look at Paul. He didn't feel like looking at Paul – that made him more ill than the dizzying spin.

How could he? Paul had worked as hard on the *Satori* as any of them. He was part of their team. Dan didn't understand a man who could pretend to be someone's friend while all along plotting against him. Part of him was a little glad it didn't make sense, but it still bothered him.

Intellectually, Dan knew that people were often dishonest, and he'd told his share of little white lies. But there was a difference between pretending to be sick from work so you could get an extra fishing day in and hiding the fact that you were about to steal and/or blow up a spaceship around a bunch of people who thought you were their friend. The betrayal struck home deeply in his heart.

Dan was lost in those thoughts, and almost missed the little glow appearing around the nose of the ship as it spun past Jupiter. Almost, but not quite – and then his attention refocused quickly. He waited for the next spin – and there it was. Traces of atmosphere reacting with the hull. He activated the radio in his helmet.

"Beth, I know you're busy right now, but I thought you should know – we're dipping into Jupiter's upper atmosphere. Seeing traces of heat reaction against the hull."

"Got that," she replied. "Switch channels and tell Andy. He's still out there, I think."

Dan fiddled with the controls for a moment to swap to channel two. "Andy?"

"Here," came the reply.

"Andy, it's about to get hot out there. You need to get yourself inside, fast."

"Can't yet, Dan. I'm still working on that last bomb. If it goes off, we're all toast."

"Can you put a rush on it? I don't know how much time you've got, but it's not a lot."

"We'll do what we can. Andy out."

Dan looked around the room, wondering what he could do to help. He unhooked himself from his seat, and drifted toward Charline's station, where she'd gotten the power running. The ship tilted again as he drifted over, and he felt gravity shove him down like a hand. The seat came rushing up at him much faster than he'd thought, and he fell against the padding with a rush of air gusting out of his lungs.

Gravity. He thought about it a moment. That meant there was already some braking action going on. The ship's aerodynamics were slowing their descent. Gas in Jupiter's upper atmosphere was reacting with their hull, generating friction and slowing them down every time the wings were flat to their angle of descent.

"I wonder if I can help that at all," he muttered. He slid into the seat and tapped the keyboard. Char's screen came up, with a new notification, saying that Majel was online and awaiting instructions.

"Nice," he said. The voice interface was still down. The emergency batteries running this console weren't giving it enough juice to manage that. But if he could type out some commands to the AI, maybe something could be done.

He tapped out the words LIST COMMAND SUMMARY.

A string of commands came up. Among them

were things he knew were offline, like the main drive.

He typed again: LIST AVAILABLE FUNCTIONAL COMMANDS.

This gave him a much shorter list. There wasn't a lot of power available, and all of the alien tech seemed offline still. Beth must be working at that. It was those alien drives that would save them, if anything could. She had to get those back online.

But there were other systems available. The *Satori*, for all that it was a starship with wormhole drives, was designed to handle planetary landings. Which meant it had been designed with aerodynamics in mind, not just space flight. Among the commands available for access were those for ailerons, flaps, and elevators.

No stick meant this was going to be tricky. He'd have to type each adjustment manually. But he'd logged a lot of hours flying, in the air as well as in space. Incrementally, he adjusted the wing and tail surface controls to counter the spin. Slowly, the crazy motion in the front window came to, if not a stop, and least a much slower slide. He put more flaps on, tilting the nose up a bit. The computer said that the *Satori* was now in a nose-up configuration for re-entry – a lot like the old shuttle craft used to use for landings on Earth.

Of course, those shuttles had never tried the routine going into Jupiter's atmosphere. He couldn't recall how fast Jupiter's winds were, but he remembered they were very fast. Things were going to get bumpy, soon, if they couldn't pull out. And warm too. The ship had good belly shielding against heat, but it was designed to land under power, using the gravity drive to control the ship's descent. The heat shielding wasn't intended to soak up the sort of heat this powerless belly-in method was going to generate. Whether the ship was torn to shreds by the wind shear or melted into slag by the heat of their atmospheric entry was moot. For the moment Dan had at least slowed the process down a little. It wasn't enough to save them.

But it was something. They were moving slower now, and gravity was pointing more or less reliably in one direction, instead of rotating as the ship spun around. He felt a brief rush of relief, relaxed his hands a little.

One wing hit a pocket of denser gas, and the ship tilted wildly off to one side. His fingers flew over the keyboard to type in a correction. That pushed the right wing back too far in the other direction, and he had to shift the ailerons a bit more to compensate. Holding this brick steady wasn't going to be easy. Dan grimaced, bringing every bit of his years of flight experience to bear on the limited controls he had. Every second he bought them gave Beth a little more time to get those engines back operational.

TWENTY-FIVE

The heat was beginning to distract Andy, even through his suit. The spinning had stopped, at least. The Satori's spin had slowed down and then finally stopped altogether. It looked like Dan had managed to do something – that had to be his handiwork. But the spinning had stopped with the ship facing right side up. Which made great sense if you were trying to use the atmosphere to break the ship's fall, but the bombs were on the bottom side of the ship, facing down toward Jupiter.

That left Andy dangling from his safety line underneath the ship as he tried to disable the last bomb. It was starting to get hot out there, even through his suit. Andy felt his body growing slick

with perspiration inside the thick protective covering. If he couldn't get that bomb free and get back
inside the ship soon, he was going to cook. And the
thing was stuck.

Not having any leverage wasn't helping, but he
had to admit most of the issue was just the metal on
metal of the bolt's connection to the ship. Perhaps
the hull was already heating up, and that was
causing expansion of the metal plates. Whatever the
cause, the bolt wasn't coming loose, not for all the
prying he could manage. So Andy pulled out a
small laser cutting tool.

"John, time for you to go back inside," Andy
said.

"Why? What are you doing with that?"

"The bomb won't come off. Going to burn
through the hull around it. But I could set it off,
trying. Don't want us both here if I do."

"How can I help?" John asked, stubbornly
staying put.

"By being where I don't need to worry about
blowing you up, OK?" Andy laughed. "That would
look bad on my resume."

John retreated back into the airlock, with some
grumbling. Once he was safely away from the blast
area Andy slowly burned away the metal in a circle

around the bomb. Ever so carefully, because if the heat of the laser warmed the bolt itself too much...!

Well, he'd been lucky to survive the first one going off. He didn't want to count on doing it twice. And even if he did, the bomb was positioned to damage the engines – which would kill their only way to escape this deathtrap.

He wished he could wipe the sweat away from his eyes. Definitely getting warmer.

"John, I might need you to haul me back in when I'm done. So don't go too far, OK?"

He heard John's steady laugh over the radio. "As if I would."

There was a temperature gauge on the inside of his helmet. He'd stopped looking at it when it passed one hundred degrees. The suit was trying to compensate for the increasing heat, but it wasn't up to the task. No space suit had been designed that would survive re-entry into an atmosphere unshielded. He tried to put the temperature out of his mind.

Instead, he kept cutting. He'd keep cutting as long as he could.

The laser was almost done with its work. Only a slim bit of metal remained. There'd be a nice hole in the hull when he was done, but that they could patch. Just another centimeter to burn through, and he'd be home free. He could drop the bolt and make his way back to the airlock. Andy's arms were burning from the effort of keeping the laser steady as the ship was buffeted around by the increasing winds.

Then he felt a pop through his fingers, and the laser went out.

"Damn it! Not now!" he said.

"What's wrong?" John asked.

"The laser died. Not meant to survive in this heat, I think. Probably fried something inside it."

"Hang tight, I'll bring another one out to you."

Andy looked at the little sliver left to cut, and the silver dollar of hull he'd almost separated around the bolt. "No, I think I might be able to pop it out now." He dropped the laser cutter – it was useless now, and he didn't have the time to put it back properly. Then he pulled out a wrench and rammed it into the gap he'd cut in the metal.

With a grunt, he hauled his legs up against the hull. Using his legs and increasing weight for leverage, he grasped the wrench with both hands, twisting and pulling against the spindle of metal left holding the bomb to the ship.

He felt it give a little.

Andy's eyes were drawn to a flashing red light in his suit helmet. The temperature indicator was giving a warning – suit temp had gone up over one hundred and twenty degrees. His breaths were coming in short, ragged gasps now as he pulled with everything he had, twisted with his arms and pushed with his legs.

And then with one last terrific effort, he broke the last of the metal. The bolt came away from the ship in his hands.

Without the metal supporting his weight, his legs pushed him off from the ship, and he plummeted down toward the planet below. He felt a brief jolt as his safety line went taut on the carabiner, but the device snapped apart, weakened by the cold and then intense heat. So he fell, and fell, and kept falling.

It felt like he'd fall forever.

And then the safety line jerked him to a halt at its full length, the spot where he'd fastened it to the airlock still holding fast. The bomb dropped from his fingers. He watched it tumble away from him, falling faster than the ship. Dan's aerobraking move had the ship falling slow enough that the bomb seemed to plummet away until it was completely out of sight. A few seconds later, a small flash lit the clouds somewhere below. Damn, that had been close.

Andy closed his eyes, too tired to contemplate climbing back up all that way. Too hot. He was having a harder and harder time breathing.

"Not so fast," came the voice over his radio. He felt a tug on his line. "I've got you!"

"John...?" he murmured.

"Hang tight. I'll get you up. Again. This better not become a habit, though!" He could hear John's familiar grin in his banter.

Andy tried to keep his breathing even and steady in the increasing heat as he felt himself begin slowly ascending toward the ship again.

TWENTY-SIX

Beth smiled. She was panting now, her air very thin. The blown seal was worse than she'd thought at first, and her suit was running through its reserves like mad. She'd exchanged the main air tank once already for the backup one that was hanging on the engine room wall – just for cases like this, where someone needed more air. But her suit was leaking too fast. The suit was trying to retain proper pressure for her, but the result was a lot of air leaking out.

So instead she'd turned down the pressure settings in her suit. She was working in the equivalent of a very high altitude environment on Earth, and her body wasn't used to it. The air leak seemed to be a little slower, anyway. The suit was compensating for less pressure loss than it had been. But the lower pressure left her feeling lightheaded, and she found it increasingly difficult to force herself to concentrate on finishing the last of these emergency repairs. More like patches than real fixes, but they would get power to where it needed to be. The rest of the damage could be cleaned up later.

But she'd gotten the job just about done. Charline had booted Majel, and Dan had been able to use the AI's assistance to right the ship, slow their descent. That had given Beth just enough breathing room to patch Majel's server directly to the alien systems. At this point, all she needed to do was flip a switch, and Majel would be linked to the main drive, wormhole drive, the alien computer bank, and whatever else was stored in that black box of tech that she'd only just begun to understand. If Charline's code could manage to connect the two, maybe Majel's program could activate the drive and get them out of there.

"Charline, it's ready," Beth said.

"You OK?" Charline asked for the hundredth time.

"No, not really. Let's get this done and get out of here."

She didn't reply, still typing on the command line interface.

Beth flipped the switch, and felt power hum through the ship. She'd restored the main power line from the engines to the human components. All over the ship, power should be coming back. They'd have consoles on the bridge. Life support would be back. They still needed engine control, though. That part was out of her hands. She looked over at Charline, still pounding console keys at a rate Beth didn't think she could have managed even without a spacesuit on.

"Power's back. Can Majel handle controls, Charline?"

"She should be able to. I've written a new program that I think will enable her to interface with the alien computer system. Maybe. It depends on how good their programming was, really; because mine is a hatchet job. And I've got her programmed to route all commands sent to her from the bridge down to the drive components."

"Somehow, it just seems wrong to be using her as a glorified wifi router, though," Beth said ruefully.

"Not really. I've managed to extrapolate a few of the the communication protocols, but if this is going to work its going to take a lot of on the fly code adaptations. Only a system as strong as Majel could handle this," Charline replied.

Beth relaxed against a wall. Her arms and legs felt like lead. She heard Charline calling over the radio net. "Dan? Majel has access to the drive system. See if you can get her to fire up the engines and get us the hell out of here!"

"Got that," Dan said back. "I'm on it."

Beth got shakily to her feet. When had she sat down? She didn't remember doing that. She'd been leaning up against the wall and then... The room was beginning to wobble around her, vision swimming. She almost fell, but Charline got a shoulder under her arm before she could.

"Thanks," Beth said in a whisper. She hadn't meant to whisper. What was wrong with her? Something about air... She was having a hard time thinking clearly.

"Hang on," Charline said, walking her over to the exit door. She swore when she saw the door, then tried poking at something on the wall next to the door, something... Beth couldn't see. Her vision was going all fuzzy now.

"That last bomb must have damaged the door,

Beth. The control panel is shot. Hang tight, going to try to force it open."

Charline set her down gently against the wall, but Beth couldn't keep her feet under her. She slid down the wall to sit on the floor – the drive must be back on, she realized. Normal gravity had set in again. Blackness was creeping around the edge of her vision.

She watched Charline tug at the door, pound on it. She saw her grab a piece of scrap metal and try to force it into the center seam where the two doors slid together and met. But the door just sat there, looking all gray and solid. The black was closing in around her sight more now, and she heard a roaring sound in her ears.

"Anyone! The doors are jammed here in the engine room," she heard Charline's voice over the radio. "I can't get them open, and Beth is leaking air. She's almost out."

Beth heard the desperate fear in her ship-mate's voice, and knew something about the situation should have bothered her, but she couldn't think clearly enough to remember what that might be. She smiled anyway. Beth couldn't see anything anymore, but she could still feel the drive through the hull, the steady thrum of her engines as they pushed back against the gravity of the giant planet below with their incomprehensible power. She'd fixed her baby, made it soar again. That asshole Paul had hurt her engines. But they were all better now, and it was time for a nap.

She closed her eyes.

TWENTY-SEVEN

D an swore under his breath as he struggled with the controls, trying to get them out of the mess they were in. His attention was split, worrying both about controlling the ship and about his friends. Andy and John were back on board, and on their way to try to help Charline and Beth out of the engine room. But Beth wasn't speaking anymore. Charline said she'd passed out. Dan wondered how much air was left in Beth's tanks. Would they be able to get the doors open in time to help her? He wanted to rush back to assist them, to do something to save her. But what could he do, wheel his chair back and stare at them while they pried the door open? No, his place was here, not back there with her…no matter what his heart was telling him, Beth's best chance for survival lay with him getting the Satori free from Jupiter's grasp.

But even that was proving problematic. They'd fallen deep enough that gravity was tugging hard at the ship. Worst of all, the main drives refused to operate at full power. Maybe Majel was just having issues with the interface, but he couldn't get enough power out of the drives to get free from the planet's pull. Dan was able to aim the ship back out of the gravity well and he was giving the engines everything he could, but it wasn't enough. They weren't even holding position – they were still slowly sinking down into the mists of Jupiter. They weren't in any danger from heat build up, going this slowly. But eventually the ship would reach a crush depth or run into a blast of hurricane force wind that would toss them off course, and that would be the end of them.

"Majel, I am running out of ideas," Dan said. And now I'm talking to a computer, he thought to himself. He looked over at Paul, but the second dose of sedatives had finally taken full effect. He had passed out a while ago. Not that Dan really wanted his company anyway. The surge of anger he felt even thinking about Paul was a distraction he didn't need. At least the computer's voice interface was active again. That gave him something to 'talk' to.

"How long until we reach crush depth?" Dan asked the computer.

"At present rate of descent, approximately thirty minutes remain until the ship reaches an atmospheric pressure which the hull cannot withstand."

Thirty minutes was more time than Beth had, from the sounds of it. But the rest of them would follow her into death if he couldn't think of something.

"Is there any way to increase power to the primary drive?" he asked.

It seemed like there was a long pause before the computer answered. "Analysis does not reveal any method at this time. Recommend diagnostic of main power conduit."

"Yeah, great. I know the main conduit is out."

Dan set up a monitor to track their progress – or backwards progress, in this case, as they slowly slipped deeper into Jupiter's soup. A heavy burst of wind buffeted the ship, and he struggled with the controls for a minute, trying to keep the ship on course. With the drives running this hot, if the nose tipped down even for a moment, they'd plummet down and be in even worse shape.

"Folks, how are things going with that door?" Dan asked.

"No luck yet, Dan. We clear of Jupiter yet?" John said over his radio.

"We're stuck. Actually, we're worse than stuck, we've slid another few hundred feet down since the engines came back. Nothing I am doing seems to be slowing us down. How's Beth? We could use her back on her feet again."

A moment passed. Dan stared at the mike. Nobody talking wasn't a very good sign. Then John said "She's still out, Dan. We're working on the door."

"I've hooked up my oxygen to her suit, buddy style," Charline said. "But it's only going to last so long."

Dan pounded his fist on his leg. Beth was going to suffocate if he didn't do something. Charline sharing her air would keep Beth alive for a little while, but when it ran out both women were going to die if they couldn't get through that door. Without Beth, repairing the damaged conduit was out of the question, and that meant there was no way to increase the engine's power. They were stuck.

"We've got a laser cutter, Dan," said Andy. "But it's a small one, not going to cut through the door too fast. We can't budge it, even with a crowbar. It's jammed."

"Got you," Dan replied. Up to him, then. And maybe...Majel. "Got an idea. Maybe. Charline? Need your help on this one."

Dan did a quick system check on the ship. Yes, all major systems seemed to be back up and functioning. More or less, anyway. He had power to everything he needed. Now all he needed to do was solve a riddle that no one had been able to solve for all the months every genius John could hire had been working on the project. Oh, and he had twenty-eight minutes. Dan rolled his eyes. No pressure.

"I'm here. What's up?" Charline said.

"You've got Majel directly interfaced with the alien computer, correct?"

"Yes."

"So does she have access to the database?"

"I think so...? I can check." There was a long pause. Then she said "Yes, relaying to your station now."

Thousands of entries whipped across his screen, each in a block of twelve incomprehensible symbols. Each symbol was color coded. He'd seen some of these before during briefings on the ship's drive. No one had been able to translate what the symbols or colors meant. Nobody had any clue, except that they seemed to be some kind of sorting system for cataloging wormhole destinations.

But Dan had an idea. They had a new data set that all those geniuses hadn't before - a new set of wormhole coordinates from the last, short jump they'd made. If the data sets were stored in any sort of rational pattern, that might just give them what they needed to solve the riddle.

"Charline, we've used the wormhole drive within this system now," Dan said.

"Yeah, I noticed," she said.

"Does the alien computer keep a log of destinations visited? We might be able to use that to get out of here."

"I don't know... I can try to write a search program for Majel to check," Charline said.

Her voice sounded hazy to Dan. He'd heard that sound before – she was losing too much oxygen to keep air in Beth's suit. That meant they were both running out of air. If Charline passed out before she could help Dan solve this, then they would be truly out of options.

"Charline, you have to focus," Dan said. "You have to get that search program running."

"I'm trying. Just…getting hard to think," Charline said. Dan could hear her shaky gasps over the radio.

He cursed under his breath. This was the solution. It had to be! Dan was certain he was right about this. But it sounded like Charline was going to pass out before she could get the program entered, and he didn't have the foggiest idea how to do it himself.

TWENTY-EIGHT

B ack when John's crews had first been tunneling out the base on the moon, there had been a cave in. A support they'd used to shore up the roof while they mined had snapped under the strain, and debris had rained down, filling the passageway. Nobody was hurt by the falling rock – but two men had been trapped on the other side. They were in spacesuits, with a few hours of air left when the rock fell.

John had been there. He personally participated in helping to move some of the rubble out of the way. The whole crew had worked in shifts, some shoring up the tunnel while others moved rocks. And he had kept on the radio through most of it, talking to the men trapped inside. He'd heard their voices growing more frightened as their air began to run down. Then he'd heard them get hazy, confused, as the oxygen level in their suits dropped and they began suffering from carbon dioxide poisoning. His crews had gotten the men out, just in time, and they'd made a rapid recovery once returned to a pressurized room. It was a near thing. John redoubled all his safety precautions for the construction crews after that event, which saved them from repeating it.

John could hear the same confusion in Charline's voice now. Her suit just wasn't able to pump out enough air for both her and Beth. By trying to give Beth some air, Charline wasn't getting enough herself.

He had listened in on Dan and Charline's conversation long enough to figure out what Dan was up to. The main drive was not getting them out. With Beth down, they weren't going to get the drive back to full power in time to do any good. Which left the wormhole drive as their last option, if Dan could somehow make it work without getting them all killed. But he was going to need Charline to make the plan work. John bowed his head, sagging forward with the weight of what he knew he had to do. If Charline couldn't get the job done, they were all dead, he reminded himself. That didn't make the call any easier. This was the price of being the leader, he reminded himself. He was the one who had to bear the weight of making the life and death decisions. Even if it meant condemning a friend to death so that the rest of them could live.

"Charline," he said into the radio, "I need you to disconnect your oxygen from Beth's suit. You're not getting enough air. We need you to be able to focus."

"John, no!" Dan said over the radio.

John ignored him. "Do it now, Charline."

"If I disconnect, Beth could die," Charline said.

"And if you pass out, we all die," John replied.

"I'm not doing it! I'm not killing her," Charline said, gasping out the last word.

"You can't do this, John. This is Beth we're talking about!" Dan said.

John slammed his fist into the wall. "Damn it, Dan! I don't want this either. But Charline's barely staying awake right now. You can hear it in her voice as well as I can. If she loses consciousness, can you save the ship without her?"

Silence over the radio.

"Well?" John's voice was furious, insistent. "Can you?"

"No," Dan's reply came back quietly.

"Then what do you think we should do?" John asked.

"That's cold, John," Dan said. John could hear the pain in his friend's voice, and it wrenched his heart. He prayed he was making the right call.

"I don't think I can do this. There has to be some other way," Charline said.

"We're out of time, Charline. We need you. You need your air. If you can't do this, none of us will survive. Including Beth," John said. "We're all in your hands."

CHARLINE BENT over Beth's still form. She held back a sob, barely. This was someone she knew! Someone who was trusting Charline to get her through this! How could she just abandon her to die? But John wasn't wrong. She could feel herself growing more light-headed by the moment. Another minute and she wouldn't be able to think clearly enough to help Dan with the computers. If she couldn't work her magic, then they were all going to die. It was the hardest thing Charline had ever had to do.

"I'm sorry, Beth," she said. Then she unclipped her buddy-breathing hose from Beth's suit.

She knew John was right. But it hurt. It hurt so much. She had her medical training from working as a volunteer on ambulance crews while she was in college. She liked the adventure – until the first person her team couldn't save. The more experienced guys said it would get better with time. But it didn't. It got worse, until she couldn't stand the guilt from not being able to help someone anymore. She quit the team and set aside any thoughts of healing people, turning her mind completely inward toward computers and the programming which made them run. If a computer died on you, well, it wasn't like it was alive. If you couldn't fix it you went and bought a new one.

As hard as the deaths those strangers had been when she worked on the ambulance, doing this felt infinitely worse. Charline hadn't known them, after all. And she'd been fighting to save them, not pulling loose the air hose that was keeping them alive. Back then she'd failed a stranger. Today Charline felt like she was murdering a friend.

Immediately, her suit pushed fresh air to her.

Charline drew in a deep breath into lungs she hadn't realized were already starting to burn from lack of oxygen. Fuzziness around her vision that she hadn't noticed began clearing as she took another few breaths.

The decision made, she forced herself to set the consequences aside. If she didn't get it together they were all going to die, and then sacrificing Beth would be for nothing. The problem Dan presented her with was complex, but not unsolvable now that she could breathe and think normally again. Charline's fingers flew over the keyboard, composing new lines of code. Majel was an enormously powerful computer. It wasn't about finding the one right communication protocol to let her search the alien computer – that would be impossible. It was about trying the entire possible range of protocols until she found one which was good enough to pass through a simple search string. She added another line to project the results up onto Dan's screen on the bridge. Then she pressed another key to execute her search.

That was all she could do. Either it would work, or it wouldn't. If the alien code was something even vaguely comprehensible to Majel's advanced hardware and software then they might have a chance. If not, Charline didn't think there was anything else they could do. Ironic, she thought, that after the struggle of so many humans to rescue the ship that the final save was up to a computer program.

TWENTY-NINE

The computer system designated Majel by its owner was not a true artificial intelligence, at least not of the sort humans had envisioned eventually creating. It was not capable of independent thought. Instead, it was just an extremely reactive, very responsive system with enormous processing power. Similar to the assistive intelligence software of decades past, Majel was a step beyond them. It was capable of analyzing data and formulating logical resolutions and plans based on available information sets.

Given a task, Majel bent its prodigious computing ability toward solving whatever the problem was which had been assigned to it. Above all else, Majel's primary directive was to answer questions and solve problems for the humans using it.

So when Charline programmed Majel to look for a log, it immediately ran a search of its own databases, looking for such a record without success. That took a microsecond, despite the terabytes of data involved. Failing that, the computer followed its algorithm for data search – to access whatever other databases were available. Usually that was the Earth's global internet, but Earth was out of reach.

The alien database, however, was right there, already hooked directly to Majel's system.

Majel began to scan the alien cubes. The interface Charline has set up was insufficient to allow a proper search, but her code gave the software some initial parameters for deducing what might be an appropriate algorithm. It adjusted for the communication issue, attempting five hundred million, sixty thousand four hundred and twenty two solutions before finding a protocol which allowed a barely adequate data transfer. There was enormous space within the database, more than Majel had access to within the entire Earth network. If she'd been alive, it would have been an exhilarating feeling. It would have been like flying through the sky after having only plodded along by foot her whole life.

The computer called Majel vaguely understood that the alien computer was responding to her database search, improving her own search functions to help her seek what she needed, improving her own processing power to help her think faster, and building new algorithms for her to help her solve the problem with which she'd been presented. Essentially the data resident within the cubes was building new code for her, extending and expanding upon her existing programming. A substantial portion of the program which was Majel now resided within the alien computer, an entirely new set of code. But in less than five seconds, she had found the answer she'd been told to seek.

DAN STARED at the computer for a few eternal moments. Every second made it less likely Beth could be rescued in time. He was about to ask Charline how long this would take when Majel came back with the answer.

"Requested log located."

Dan leaned in toward the screen. "Display," he said.

A string of twelve results scrolled up the screen. "That's it?" he asked.

"Records indicate database was uploaded and the list restarted before these entries."

"So they wiped the list when they reported in where they'd been."

No response. Seemed like the computer didn't read that as a question. Dan scanned the list, the log entries of the last dozen jumps this ship had made. Most of those jumps had happened so long ago in the past that it was almost incomprehensible to him. There at the bottom of the list, sure enough, Dan saw two identical sequences of symbols. No, not quite the same. The symbols themselves were ever so slightly different. But the color patterns were identical, or really close to being identical. It was difficult to know if the shading being displayed on his screen was precisely what the stored colors represented.

Yellow-Blue-Blue-Green-Red-Red-Red-White

He looked at the entry immediately before the last two.

Yellow-Blue-Green-Green-Green-Red-White-White

No clue what it all meant. Maybe they could figure it out later. But the two identical ones were mostly likely the ship jumping into this solar system, and then his jump out to Jupiter within the same system. He couldn't use those. If he was right, the wormholes were a little like riding a bicycle. Pedal the bike fast, and it went straight without any trouble. But pedal slowly – put less power into the wormhole, like they did for a very short jump – and the bike wobbled. Then a big gravity well could bend the wormhole.

Try to jump right to Earth from Jupiter, and they could end up right next to the sun instead, as the sun's gravity yanked their wormhole off course.

But if they jumped out, then they could jump back...!

That third entry should be for whatever system the ship came from.

A thousand years ago.

No telling what would be there after all these years. Maybe a thriving civilization. Maybe a bunch of aliens waiting to blow them out of the sky. But he was out of other ideas, and Beth was almost out of time. He glanced at the gauge for the ship's descent, and saw that the ship wasn't doing so well, either. They were really getting quite deep into Jupiter's soup.

He hit the intercom to call all radios on the ship. "Andy, any luck with that door yet?"

"Working on burning through, Dan, but it's slow going. We're doing our best – got a small hole now."

"Right. OK, I want everyone to hold onto something. Turn off the laser cutter. I've got an idea I'm going to try."

"Something crazy?" John asked.

"Yeah, John. Something crazy." Indeed.

"Good luck."

Dan shut off the channel. They'd all do their best to brace themselves. Time to focus.

"Majel, can you plug the coordinates for the third to last entry into the wormhole drive?"

"Affirmative."

"Do so. Stand by to execute wormhole on my command."

The wormhole drive created a hole in space in front of the ship, and they were going backwards, sliding down into Jupiter's gravity. He'd have to turn the ship around to get some forward motion. Fingers flying over his keyboard, he entered a string of commands. Then he used single keystrokes to gently lower the nose down. Working to keep the wings level while he dropped the nose was a struggle – the wind wanted to wrest control away from him, was fighting him every moment.

The nose slipped down, and they were flying forward again – deeper into Jupiter's soup!

Dan couldn't believe he was doing this again. He couldn't think of any other options though, and Beth was the only person who might have come up with a better solution. Beth, who was locked in with her engines, suffocating.

His mouth a grim line, he paused his fingers over the keyboard. "Majel, are we set for jump to the coordinates I specified?"

"Affirmative."

"Execute."

He'd seen it before, so the shock of the worm-hole was gone. The powerful beam shot from the front of the ship, opening a hole in the fabric of space. This time, he tried to pay attention to the flashing colors as they coruscated around the ship, but it was too much. Too bright, too many colors and patterns exploding one after another. The wormhole spiraled open in front of the *Satori* like a door opening in the universe, welcoming her home. She danced forward on the main drive, and left Jupiter far, far behind.

THIRTY

The *Satori* sang her way out of the wormhole in a burst of light and sound. Dan recovered faster this time, staying focused on keeping control of the ship as they re-entered realspace God only knew where. Beth was still suffocating in the airless engine room, her space suit damaged by one of the blasts. She needed him. He couldn't let her down.

That thought snapped him fully back to reality. He scanned the board in front of him, and was surprised to find that the ship had already brought up a detailed plot of the solar system they'd entered. It was definitely not the one they'd been in moments before. He could only see six planets on the image;

the *Satori* was in a tight orbit of the second planet out from the star.

"Majel, pull up the record of wormhole jumps," Dan said.

The ship's AI complied, and his screen was full of those curiously colored symbols again. This time, there was a new addition – the jump they'd just made. Which meant the one before it was their jump from Luna to Jupiter. And he was betting the one before that was the ship's jump to Earth, around a thousand years ago. It was a gamble. He was pretty sure they'd end up in his home system, but the destination point might not be close enough to Earth to matter. It was the best chance he could think to get Beth back to Earth before she asphyxiated.

"Majel, get ready for a wormhole jump to the third most recent coordinates," he said.

"Wormhole drive has insufficient power to comply. Drive will have adequate power in fifty-eight minutes."

"Damn it!" Dan cried out. That was too long. Beth would be dead long before that timer ran out. "Why so long?"

"The most recent wormhole drive activation drained engine capacitors of nearly their full

charge. Time to restore enough power for the specified trip: fifty-seven minutes and forty seven
seconds."

Dan's hands were sweating. He glanced at the
scanner, which was continuing to put out more
information about the system's planets. One was a
small ball close to the star. Four were gas or frozen
planets, pretty far out. But the planet the *Satori*
orbited looked remarkably Earth-like. Complete
with a breathable atmosphere, according to the data
scrolling by his screen. His heart leaped, hope
thrilling through him.

"Majel, is this scan data current information? I
didn't think we had the ability to get this much
detail."

"Scan data is from the alien components of the
ship."

"And they're saying the atmosphere will support
human life."

"Affirmative."

He swore under his breath. The wormhole drive
would never be ready in time to save Beth. But a
dive into the breathable atmosphere of this planet
might do the trick. Air ought to flow back into the
Satori through the same holes that it had escaped
through, filling the engine room with the oxygen

Beth needed so badly. Dan decided he was feeling like a bird in the hand sort of guy today.

"Cancel wormhole, Majel." He accelerated and banked the ship toward the planet. They rocketed into the upper atmosphere at high speed. Every second counted, so he poured on all the power the engines could give him.

Suddenly, little red dots were showing up on his radar. According to the display, they were all actively pinging the ship with some kind of sensors of their own. He tapped the display. Those were satellites! Someone had a satellite network orbiting this world. Maybe there would be life down there on the planet below them. Perhaps even the alien's who'd made their ship's drive in the first place.

"Majel, anything you can tell me about those satellites down there?" Incredible. Intellectually, he knew that the existence of the *Satori* was pretty solid proof of life beyond his home solar system. But knowing that was one thing. Seeing active satellites so far away from home was another thing entirely!

"Multiple active sensor networks suggest probable defense devices."

That sounded very bad. Dan watched the satellites as they continued pinging away. "Nothing to see here. Just passing through," he muttered under his breath. He was going to pass awful close to a couple of them. They were in orbits spread all around the planet.

"Launch detected from satellite," Majel warned.

Dan glanced back at the screen. "Well, there goes the wishing they were friendly." Then he groaned. The cloaking device! He snapped it on and brought the ship into a canopy roll, dropping the nose straight toward the ground as he exited the roll. The missile zipped by through the space they would have occupied if he hadn't swerved.

"Good at tracking. Not so good at spotting invisible ships. Score one for us!" He should have put the cloak up as soon as the ship came out of the wormhole. It was hard to get used to the idea of making one's ship invisible, he thought ruefully.

They were getting deeper into the planet's atmosphere. He checked *Satori's* gauges. Was it enough? Yes! Air was already refilling the engine room, pressure driving back up toward normal levels.

"Charline, you've got air in there again. Get Beth's suit open!" Be in time, he thought. Please, let him have moved fast enough.

"Will do!" she said over the radio.

"We'll be through the engine room door soon," Andy added.

Not soon enough, though. Dan knew Andy was trying his best, but the laser cutter wouldn't have gotten through in time. He just had to hope that he'd been quick enough to make the jump, and fast enough in getting the ship down toward the planet, and that Charline had been able to get Beth's helmet off all right. Dan hated being up in the front, far from where he could do anything more.

"I've got her helmet off, Dan," Charline said. "You did it! She's breathing. Beth is going to be OK."

Dan sagged against his console in relief. He reached out a hand to cup his face, shaking a little in reaction to the news and all the terrible turmoil which had led up to that moment. Thank god. He'd managed to save her. Dan hadn't realized until he saw her back on the moon how important that woman still was to him. He hadn't really thought about her in years. But seeing her again, even after all that time, brought back the memories of everything they had shared.

And then he'd thought he was going to lose her all over again. For good, this time, without any chance of seeing her again someday. Dan realized he would have done just about anything to keep Beth safe. He didn't know what that made her to him, except that she was still someone he cared about. Probably more than he cared about himself.

The *Satori* sailed on through the clouds, diving closer toward the ground. Landing seemed like a good idea. The ship needed repairs, and those would be easier once they were on the ground. Now, Dan could see that while those clouds looked normal from above, they were dust storms rather than water vapor. The rest of the planet only vaguely resembled his homeworld. The mess below him looked a little like Earth, if it had been scoured to bedrock and someone's sewer poured in to replace the water. The ocean he passed over was black, with some sort of glossy coating. The land, if anything, was worse. Huge impact craters were everywhere. No telling what the terrain used to be like. Now it was barren, broken, and deserted. This planet might have air humans could breathe, but Dan couldn't see a single sign of life anywhere.

And then he passed over one particularly tall crater wall, and everything changed.

A SPECIAL SNIPPET FROM BOOK 2:
STELLAR LEGACY

The Satori's engine room had taken the brunt of the damage from Paul's explosives. Two of the small bombs had detonated, tearing up the deck, shattering plates and sending debris showering around the room. The main conduit running power from the alien engine to the rest of the ship was still shredded. A patch cable allowed some power and control, but they had a lot of repair work to do before the ship was going to be back to full power.

Charline was kneeling in the middle of the floor, holding Beth's still form and crying when John and Andy pushed the door into the engine room the rest of the way loose. Both women had their spacesuit helmets off. The holes torn in the hull had allowed enough breathable air to pass through that they could survive without the suit air. Andy's efforts with the laser cutter had finally worked, burning away the twisted metal that pinned the steel safety door shut. With a final, concerted heave, they were through. John froze in the doorway a moment, taking in the tableau. Then he made to step forward to help.

But Charline was on her feet before John took a single step into the room. She flung her suit helmet at him. It hit his chest, rebounded against the floor and spun there. Before it stopped spinning she was already moving toward him. Charline took a hard swing with a right hook, her fist slamming into the left side of his face. John toppled sideways, falling back against the door frame.

"You bastard!" she hissed. "Don't you ever tell me to do something like that again!" She stepped in and hammered blows against John's chest with each word. Andy slipped in at her side, as if to comfort her, but John put up a hand and forestalled him.

"I understand that I asked you to do a terrible thing, Charline. But we all would have died if you hadn't been able to connect Majel to the wormhole records. You kept all of us from burning up in Jupiter's atmosphere." John looked Charline straight in the eyes, and even through her anguish she could hear the compassion in his voice. "It was the right call. Hard, but right."

Charline knew that he was right, but that didn't make it easier to have cut off a friend's air. Beth's suit had been damaged in an explosion. The woman had continued working right up until she passed out. Charline had kept her alive by hooking Beth up to her own tank, using her air for both of them. But her suit couldn't put out enough air to keep them both breathing and compensate for the leak in Beth's suit. Charline was heading toward passing out herself when John ordered her to cut off Beth's air.

And she'd gone along with it. She'd done as she was told. The guilt Charline felt over that decision was unbearable. She felt Andy's arm behind her back, lending her support, and her hands went still on John's chest. She could understand, but she couldn't forgive.

"And if she'd died?" Charline asked.

John looked over Charline then, to Andy, then back into her eyes. "Then at least we would have been alive to mourn her."

She felt Andy's strong hands begin to lead her away. She turned, ready to start in on him, but then she saw the look on his face. She knew in an instant that at some point, he'd been in her shoes. He'd faced a moment where he had sacrificed someone he cared about for the good of others. Where he'd placed the need of the many over the needs of one person right there in front of him. He knew how much she was hurting. Charline could see it in his eyes. Somehow that shared pain made her own agony a little less.

Her need to be understood overwhelmed her anger in an instant, and Charline collapsed against Andy, crying.

Beth's too-still form lay on the engine room deck, helmet off to one side where Charline had set it down. Charline's medical scanner lay on her chest, a green light pulsing softly.

"So she's...?" John couldn't finish the question.

Charline sobbed again, trying to pull herself together. "She's alive."

She turned from Andy to glare at John. "No thanks to you. I hooked the buddy breathing up after I finished the program. Didn't care what you'd say."

Charline was still furious, but felt it wash away from her as she looked over at Beth. "I don't know how much it helped. By the time Dan said I could take her helmet off, she wasn't breathing. I don't know for how long. Her heart was still beating. I did rescue breathing until she started breathing on her own again."

Andy offered her a hand again, and she took it. "Let's get her to the infirmary," Andy said.

"Yes. She's stable now, but she'll be more comfortable there," Charline said.

Andy carefully knelt beside the unconscious women and lifted her gently into his arms. Charline felt a little bit of the weight she'd been carrying leave her shoulders as Andy took on the load. She'd done all she could. Now there were others who would help. Over and over, trapped inside the engine room Charline had wondered if she had done the right thing, detaching her air supply from Beth's suit. Surely she could have finished the coding without doing that! Then Beth would have been fine. There'd be no questions about how quickly she would recover from the ordeal. Also no crushing sense of guilt for what she had done.

Charline couldn't help but stare at Beth's still form. There was nothing she could do but hope the other woman would be all right. Then Andy turned and met her gaze. The understanding she saw in his eyes warmed her heart and for a moment dispelled some of her remorse.

"Come on, let's get her cleaned up and resting. Then we need to make sure the ship is spaceworthy again," Andy said. "The sooner we get the Satori fixed, the sooner we can all go home."

Charline flashed him a weak smile and followed Andy out of the engine room. Far as she was concerned, she'd follow him anywhere.

GET THE BOOK TODAY: http://mybook.to/satori2

Exclusive free story for fans of Kevin McLaughlin's science fiction! Learn the story of how John found the alien ship on the moon, launching the adventure which spans the stars and saves all of humanity!
https://dl.bookfunnel.com/ab58935k8u

KEVIN'S NOTES

Thank you for reading this book. I hope you've enjoyed the journey, and I can't tell you how grateful I am that you've read it all the way to the end, and that you're reading these notes now as well.

I first wrote the Satori stories contained in this book, Ad Astra, and the sequel Stellar Legacy, back in early 2014. They were published around the middle of the year as a five part serial, and then merged into two novellas in August of 2016. Since then the Satoriverse has grown. I've added a number of new novels: Deep Waters, No Plan Survives Contact, Liberty, Satori's Legacy, Ashes of War, and Embers of War. The final two books will be coming out late 2024 and early 2025 respectively, if all goes as planned. That will wrap the series up at fifteen total books.

So why this book now? Why an "author's preferred edition"? What the heck does that mean, anyway?

Since I first wrote this story, I've penned over a million new words of fiction. I've grown as an author over those years. I've learned a ton about storytelling. I've gotten better at this gig, and Ad Astra was sitting there as a vestige of my old writing quality, without the depth of emotion that I've learned to add. I decided it was time to do something about it.

The original Ad Astra was about 26,000 words. This new book is over 40,000 words. It's still a short novel, but that's how I prefer to write: concise, keeping the plot tight and the story direct. Lots of action, lots of adventure...but I wanted to add more time with each character, and I wanted to increase the emotional depth of the work for both new readers and old fans alike.

What you've got here is the result of that effort. I think it's a phenomenal improvement over the original. I've added more background detail for some of the characters. There's more internal monologue and dialogue between the characters.

It's just a better story for having the additional space to tell it in. There's a little less madcap sprinting from one scene of danger to the next. As my mother would put it, there's less of a sense of the "Perils of Pauline" going on, and more time to get to know the cast.

I hope you've enjoyed this book. I've gotten a few smiles - and made myself groan a few times - going over that old writing and polishing it up to make it new again. Stellar Legacy and Deep Waters (books two and three) will be getting the same gentle tune-up, and both books will be much improved for the effort.

I'd also like to thank my incredible ARC team for their final push to help make this book the best it can possibly be. Especially the select team who pitched in by spotting the last couple of typos that were missed by the editor! Thank you, B. Allen, Linda C., Gary B., Andrew R., Darica C., Ron G., Suseanne G., and Michael S.! Your contributions were all incredibly valuable. Getting the final typos out of a book is a pain in the neck, and you all helped save the day.

There's a lot more story to come. I plan for at least twelve novels in the series before it is completed, and who knows? There may be more.

The universe these characters are only just beginning to explore in this story is a very large one, filled with danger and beauty, adventure and tragedy. There's plenty of room for a great many stories in the years to come.

If you've enjoyed this tale, please leave a review! I read every one of them, and they help inform my process. I love hearing from readers, either via email at kevins.studio@gmail.com, or through your reviews on Amazon. Before this rewrite, in fact, I went back over every single review on the first book, looking for issues to address during the process. Your reviews made this story better. Thank you.

One last note: I have a short Satori adventure available only to fans. It's not available for sale on any vendor. The tale is all about how John stumbled across the alien ship in the first place, and what he did when he found it. You can get the short story, "Finding Satori", by signing up for my email list here: https://www.instafreebie.com/free/Uor9d

Thanks again so much for your reading, your time, and your reviews. I wouldn't be a writer without you.

The Adventures of the Starship Satori:

Ad Astra
Stellar Legacy
Deep Waters
No Plan Survives Contact
Liberty
Satori's Destiny
Ashes of War
Embers of War
Iron and Dust

ABOUT THE AUTHOR

USA Today bestselling author Kevin McLaughlin has written more than three dozen science fiction and fantasy novels, along with more short stories than he can easily count. Kevin can be found most days in downtown Boston, working on the next novel. His bestselling Blackwell Magic fantasy series, Accord science fiction series, Valhalla Online LitRPG series, and the fan-favorite Starship Satori series are ongoing.

I love hearing from readers!

www.kevinomclaughlin.com
kevins.studio@gmail.com